A FATAL REUNION

John Dennison died quietly, the silence disturbed only by the sound of his legs threshing the bed-sheets as the man astride his chest choked the life out of him.

DCI Millson suspects the killer as Albert Smedley, Irene Smedley's jealous husband who had earlier been heard quarrelling violently with his wife in the flat below Dennison's. His suspicions are strengthened when he discovers Irene Smedley had lied to him about how she'd spent her time the night before the murder.

Then other information comes to light and DCI Millson and DS Scobie begin unravelling a story that leads back into the past, when four young girls swore an oath of secrecy about what happened one Christmas night during the Second World War. But can the police break the conspiracy of silence before another murder is committed?

A FATAL
REUNION

Malcolm Forsythe

HarperCollins*Publishers*

Collins Crime
An imprint of HarperCollins*Publishers*
77–85 Fulham Palace Road, London W6 8JB

First published in Great Britain
in 1995 by Collins Crime

1 3 5 7 9 10 8 6 4 2

© Malcolm Forsythe 1995

Malcolm Forsythe asserts the moral right to be
identified as the author of this work

A catalogue record for this book is
available from the British Library

ISBN 0 00 232540 3

Set in Meridien and Bodoni

Photoset by Rowland Phototypesetting Ltd
Bury St Edmunds, Suffolk
Printed and bound in Great Britain by
HarperCollinsManufacturing Glasgow

A FATAL REUNION

CHAPTER 1

John Dennison died quietly, the silence disturbed only by the sound of his legs threshing the bedsheets as the man astride his chest choked the life out of him.

It had been raining slightly when John Dennison left his office at five o'clock. He joined the rush-hour crowd pouring into the underground at Oxford Circus and squeezed into a crowded eastbound train on the Central Line.

As the doors closed he was confined under the curve of the roof between the door and a man in a bowler hat. The man was short and the brim of his hat caught under John Dennison's nose as the compacted passengers swayed rhythmically with the movement of the train. John reckoned bowler hats should be banned on the tube, along with stiletto heels that pierced your shoes when women trod on your toes in the crush.

At Holborn, passengers spilled out onto the platform. More passengers surged in and the man in the bowler hat was swept away down the carriage. As the bodies rearranged themselves a girl's hair brushed John Dennison's mouth. The doors closed on the second attempt and pressed the girl's curves firmly against him. It was much pleasanter than having a bowler hat prodding his face, but she only lasted to the next station. After that he was trapped in a group of garlic-breathing men all the way to Liverpool Street.

At Liverpool Street he caught the 5.30 train to Colchester and sat reading the evening paper for a while. As the train rattled through Romford he laid it aside and reflected on his Job Appraisal Review that morning. John felt that at twenty-four it was time he moved on from the work he was doing, and he had said so.

'Well . . . let's see,' said his Head of Division, turning the pages of a report in front of him. 'You certainly seem to have done an excellent job arranging the reunion.'

John Dennison was secretary of the department's Retired Staff Association and had recently organized a reunion to mark the fiftieth anniversary of the evacuation of two hundred of its staff to Bournemouth during the London blitz.

Tracing the evacuees had not been easy. Some had been killed in the war, some had not returned to the department after it, and some had died since. He'd begun by researching the personnel division's confidential files in archives and then visiting last known addresses and asking questions.

Gradually, as he located survivors and they gave him addresses of others they'd kept in touch with, he built up a file of information and personal histories and eventually tracked down thirty-five of the original two hundred. Twenty-six of them attended a reunion at the Wessex Hotel in Bournemouth on 12th November 1990 – fifty years to the day a special train had left Waterloo station carrying them to safety.

At the end of the interview that morning, the Head of Division had said, 'You'll be pleased to know I'm recommending you for promotion to another post.'

John was delighted. He hoped his girlfriend, Sarah, would be impressed. He had mixed feelings about Sarah Howarth. Their relationship hadn't progressed since they met three months ago and he didn't understand why. He liked her a lot and she seemed to like him, yet she kept him at arm's length. He couldn't make her out.

The train drew in to Colchester at a quarter to seven and by seven o'clock he'd walked up the hill to his flat in Mile End Road and was cooking a supper of sausages and chips.

At nine o'clock he put on his coat and started down

the stairs to the front door. The house was a post-war semi-detached and had been converted to two flats. The downstairs flat was occupied by his landlady, Irene Smedley, who owned the house.

As he descended the stairs the door of her flat opened and she stood in the doorway looking up at him, the hall light catching her blonde hair. She was wearing a black leather skirt and a white blouse with a scoop neck. John thought she was about thirty but, in fact, Irene Smedley was approaching her fortieth birthday.

'Going out?' Her lips parted in a smile.

He nodded.

'Got your front door key?' She leaned towards him as he reached the foot of the stairs, the scoop neck sagging forward to reveal the lace tops of a half-cup bra.

He nodded again.

'Not that I'd mind if you knocked me up,' she said, her smile widening.

He grinned to show he understood the innuendo and opened the front door.

Raising her hand, she wiggled her fingers in a farewell gesture. 'Be good,' she said. 'And if you can't be good be careful.'

In the early hours of the morning, a gloved hand inserted a screwdriver between the two halves of the sash window in the hall and forced open the catch. The bottom half of the window was quietly raised and a dark figure put a leg over the sill and climbed in.

The man stood listening for a moment then crept along the hall and up the stairs. He listened again outside the door to the bedroom on the landing then gently turned the handle and stepped inside.

In the gloom he moved silently to the bed and stood listening to John Dennison's regular breathing. Quietly, he eased a plastic bag from his pocket. Then, in one swift movement, he straddled the sleeping man and pulled the bag over his head. Closing his hands viciously on his

7

victim's throat, he sealed the bag around his neck with encircling fingers.

Dazed with sleep, arms pinned beneath the bedclothes by his attacker's knees, John Dennison was helpless in the relentless grip of the man crouching over him. As he struggled for breath, the clinging plastic was sucked in over his nose and mouth and he quickly suffocated.

Detective Chief Inspector George Millson was in a bad mood. He'd been listening to a programme about single parents on his car radio. Why was it, he complained to himself as he turned off the roundabout at Colchester station into Mile End Road, that everyone thought single parents were young, female, and with small children? Public sympathy, and the help and facilities, were all directed to this one group. A man like him . . . nearing forty and struggling to bring up a thirteen-year-old daughter on his own . . . needed help and advice too sometimes. Yet he wasn't even counted in the statistics of single parents because he didn't receive State benefit.

It had been a joyful day for George Millson when his daughter, Dena, chose to live with him instead of with her mother and new husband, and they had managed fine together in the year she'd been with him. Lately, though, Dena had become difficult and this morning they'd had an argument over a girlfriend she'd brought home yesterday evening.

Usually, he didn't pay much attention to the girls Dena was friendly with. Some had weird hairdos and wore tattered denim shorts, but otherwise they seemed normal youngsters to him.

Julie was different. Alarm bells began ringing the moment he set eyes on her, or rather the moment he noticed the way she looked at him. He'd seen that predatory look before. In the eyes of underage girls taken into custody for their own protection. He made the mistake of speaking out.

'You only saw her for a second!' Dena said fiercely when

he expressed disapproval of Julie over breakfast. 'You can't possibly know what she's like in that time. Anyway, she's fun and I like her.'

'What's her family like? Have you met them?' That had been another mistake, greeted with an angry pout.

'No, and I don't care about her family!'

Which made him fear the worst. And as usual when they had a tiff, he was denied a parting kiss when he delivered her to school that morning.

Detective Sergeant Norris Scobie was already at the murder scene when Millson arrived. Unlike the chief inspector, Scobie was cheerful. Yesterday evening, over a candle-lit dinner in the Black Dog at Tanniford, he and his girlfriend, Kathy Benson, had agreed to set up home together. They still had to resolve which of them would move in with the other: whether he would give up his flat in Colchester or whether Kathy would let her flat over the estate agent's in Tanniford and move in with him.

Scobie would have liked them both to sell their flats and move into a larger one, but Kathy was against that.

'The market's depressed,' she said. 'Take it from me, it's a bad time to sell.' And, since she was an estate agent, he couldn't argue.

In John Dennison's flat a photographer was taking pictures of the body on the bed and a scene of crime officer was scouring the bedclothes for hairs and fibres.

'Who is he?' Millson asked Scobie, peering at the hooded figure on the bed.

'His name's John Dennison. He works in the Home Office. He's the secretary of their Retired Staff Association apparently. The police surgeon reckons death occurred between five and ten hours ago. And the place has been thoroughly turned over.'

'Uh-huh. Who found the body?'

'His landlady – Irene Smedley. She lives downstairs. His office telephoned her when he didn't show up for work this morning and she came upstairs and found him like this.'

9

'The pathologist?'

'On his way,' Scobie said.

'Right. We'll have a word with the landlady while we're waiting.'

Irene Smedley eyed the two policemen speculatively as she opened her door and they introduced themselves. She had a fondness for policemen – the ones she saw in television dramas, that is. Especially hard-looking ones like George Millson with his short dark hair and a blue shadow round his chin as though he hadn't shaved lately. And she wouldn't mind having her bell rung by the tall sergeant with the copper-coloured hair, she told herself.

'Married, but separated,' she informed Millson as they followed her into a sitting room. She had a glass of whisky in her hand and a small cigar between her lips.

'Sit yourselves down. Drink?' She made for a well-stocked cocktail cabinet.

'Thank you, no,' Millson said.

'Well, I'll just have a top-up.' She replenished her glass and sat down, the black leather skirt riding up above her knees.

'A dreadful, dreadful shock it's been.' She took a gulp of whisky. 'Gave me a real turn.'

'What time was it when you found the body?' Scobie asked.

'Body?' She shook her head mournfully. 'Yes, I suppose that's all he is now – a body, poor boy. Time? Well, his office phoned about ten and I went straight up there and found him.' The memory brought moisture to her eyes. 'Such a nice boy. He looked awful . . . lying there . . . that bag over his head . . .' She broke off, shuddering. 'When did it happen?'

'In the early hours of the morning probably. Why? Did you hear anything?'

'No . . . oh no. I just wondered.'

'How well did you know him?' Millson asked.

She drew on the cigar, inhaling deeply. 'He used to come down for a drink now and again and we'd chat a

bit. He cut the grass for me . . . I sewed his buttons on
. . . things like that. So I suppose I knew him quite well.'

'Was he home yesterday evening?'

'Not all evening. He went out in his car about nine
o'clock and came in again at ten.'

'Do you know where he went?' Millson asked.

'No, no idea.'

'Was he alone when he came in?'

'Oh yes,' she said confidently and Millson suspected
Irene Smedley had taken a close interest in her young
lodger.

'Did you notice anything after that? Hear any noises?'
Scobie asked.

'Well, I heard Johnny on the phone soon after he came
in. Very angry, he was.'

Millson's interest quickened. 'Did you hear what he
said?'

'No, 'fraid not.'

'What about earlier in the evening?' Millson asked.
'Before Mr Dennison went out. Anything happen then?'

She shook her head. 'Nothing out of the way.'

There was a knock on her door and a uniformed
constable put his head round it. 'The pathologist's
arrived, sir.'

Millson stood up. 'Thank you, Mrs Smedley. We may
need to ask some more questions later.'

'Yes, OK,' she said. 'Any time.'

Outside in the hall Millson said, 'Have a word with the
neighbours, Norris, and see if they know anything.'

When Millson re-entered the upstairs bedroom the
pathologist, David Duvall, was pulling on surgical gloves
and giving instructions to the photographer. He nodded to
Millson then bent over the body on the bed and carefully
removed the plastic bag from its head. He stepped back
for the photographer to take pictures of Dennison's face
and laid the bag on the bed. It was the kind of bag used
to package domestic goods like electric kettles and toasters.

Duvall smoothed the wrinkles from the bag for the

photographer who then refocused and took a close-up of the printing on it.

WARNING: *Keep away from children and dispose of safely. This bag can cause suffocation if placed over the head.*

Duvall smiled at the irony. 'And that's just what it did do, I imagine.'

'So it's definitely murder?' Millson asked.

'Oh no, not necessarily. Could be suicide. You swallow a handful of sleeping pills, put a plastic bag over your head and drift off peacefully. Works quite well. Or it could be an accident – that is, if you're that way inclined and get sexual pleasure from half suffocating yourself. Brings on wonderful hallucinations, I'm told. Trouble is, it's risky – especially if you tie yourself up as well. Let's take a look at him.'

The pathologist eased down the bedclothes and uncovered the pyjama-clad body. 'Well, this chap didn't do that.' He moved to the head of the bed and raised John Dennison's eyelids in turn. 'Petechial haemorrhages . . . asphyxiation all right,' he announced.

Straightening, he lifted the hands and examined the fingernails. 'If he was murdered, it doesn't look as though he was able to put up a struggle.' He lowered the hands and turned to Millson. 'Tell you more when I've had him on the slab.'

'Would there have been much noise?' Millson asked.

'I doubt it, with that bag over his head.'

As Duvall began supervising the preparation of the body for removal, Scobie appeared in the doorway.

'One lot of neighbours are away on holiday,' he told Millson, 'but the woman right next door says Mrs Smedley's husband was here yesterday evening and they were shouting and screaming at each other. It was a real ding-dong apparently. She says it was about Mrs Smedley's carryings-on. According to her, Irene Smedley has an eye for the men.'

12

'That wouldn't surprise me,' Millson said. 'Let's have another word with her.'

Downstairs, they found Irene Smedley sipping black coffee and smoking another cigar.

'We understand from a neighbour your husband was here yesterday evening, Mrs Smedley, and the two of you were quarrelling,' Millson said.

'That nosy cow next door, I suppose. Yes, Bert and me had a bit of a bat.'

'What about?'

She glared at him. 'What's that got to do with anything?'

'Please answer the question,' he said.

She shrugged. 'Bert thinks he still has rights over me . . . thinks he can tell me what to do. He don't like me going out and enjoying myself.'

'With anyone in particular?'

She smiled broadly. 'Anything in trousers. Talking to the milkman used to set him off when he lived here.'

'What time did he leave last night?'

'About ten, a bit before Johnny came in.'

'What did you do then?'

Her eyes flicked away from him. 'Nothing much. Watched telly mostly.'

Scobie put in a question. 'And you didn't hear anything during the night? No sounds from upstairs?'

Her eyes slid sideways. 'To tell you the truth, Sergeant, I was stoned . . . pie-eyed . . . when I went to bed. My old man had been carrying on at me, winding me up, for the best part of an hour. When he left I downed a few whiskies then climbed into bed and went out like a light.'

'Did Mr Dennison have a girlfriend?' Millson asked.

'Yeah, Sarah. Sarah Howarth. She lives in Ipswich. She phoned me this morning when she couldn't get Johnny at his office, and I told her what had happened. She said she's coming over.'

Scobie, busily writing, asked, 'And do you know who his next of kin are?'

13

'His parents, I suppose. They live in Eastbourne.'

'And your husband's address, please?'

Her eyes flashed with alarm. 'What d'you want that for?'

'We shall need to speak to him,' Scobie told her.

'Oh, he won't like that.'

'Too bad,' Millson said sourly. 'Give the sergeant his address.'

She gave an address near Halstead.

As they returned upstairs Millson said, 'Unless I'm mistaken, Norris, Mrs Smedley fancied young Dennison. I don't know if that led to anything, but it's possible he was the cause of the row with her husband. Go and see him when we've finished here. Ask him about the quarrel and make sure he can account for his movements after he left here last night.'

Sarah Howarth arrived not long after John Dennison's body had been taken away to the mortuary. A WPC intercepted her as she tried to enter the house and another WPC notified Millson. He came out to see her, buttoning up his coat against the March wind.

'I'm John's girlfriend,' Sarah told him. 'Mrs Smedley said she found John dead in bed this morning. What happened?'

Millson regarded her curiously. Her voice was flat and unemotional and she showed no signs of distress. Fair, wavy hair flowed from under the Cossack hat and over the upturned collar of her coat. She had high, arched eyebrows. They gave her face a detached expression as though her thoughts were elsewhere.

'All I can tell you at the moment, Miss Howarth, is that Mr Dennison has been found dead and we're treating his death as suspicious.'

'He *was* murdered, though, wasn't he? Mrs Smedley said he'd been suffocated.'

'We'll know more after the postmortem.'

'It has to be murder, though, doesn't it?' she persisted.

Millson had no intention of repeating the pathologist's other suggestions. 'There's no more to be said until we have the results of the postmortem,' he said firmly.

'I see. Is there anything I can do to help?'

'Yes, if you wouldn't mind answering a few questions for me. Did Mr Dennison have a date with you last night?'

'No, why?'

'He went out in his car at nine and came back about

15

ten. If he wasn't meeting you, do you know where he went?'

'No, I've no idea.'

'When did you last see him?'

'The day before yesterday. We went to the theatre.'

'Have you spoken to him since – on the telephone perhaps?'

'No, that was the last time we spoke.'

'Only Mrs Smedley has told us she heard him having an argument with someone on the phone soon after he came in last night.'

'Well, it wasn't with me.' Her tone was suddenly curt.

'And his flat seems to have been thoroughly searched. Do you know if he had anything especially valuable?'

She shook her head. 'Not that I know of.'

'One last question, Miss Howarth. Was he in trouble of any kind?'

She smiled thinly. 'John was a rather dull civil servant. And very careful . . . about everything. I can't imagine him ever getting into trouble.'

Bert Smedley lived in an isolated cottage on a side road off the A131 between Halstead and Sudbury. A sign in carved lettering on the gatepost of the cottage read:

ALBERT SMEDLEY
MAKER OF FINE FURNITURE

There was little in the way of fine furniture on view when Norris Scobie entered the dilapidated shed at the rear of the cottage. He'd walked up a cart track from the road and past the cottage with its neglected garden to the shed behind. There was timber stacked against it and from inside came the whine of an electric saw.

Smedley, with a pencil behind his ear and wearing a carpenter's apron, was bent over a steel bench guiding a thick oak plank through a sawing machine. He was a heavily built man of about forty-five and totally bald

16

except for a few long strands of brown hair which flopped across his head from a tuft at the crown.

Scobie shouted from the doorway, but the noise of the machine drowned his voice. He picked his way forward past a drilling machine and through a jungle of partly completed pieces of furniture.

Smedley suddenly became aware of him. Reaching up, he switched off the electric saw.

'Who are you? And what you doing creeping up on me like that?' He spoke in the dialect of north Essex, different from the accent around the Thames estuary.

'Detective Sergeant Scobie.' Scobie showed his warrant card.

'What d'you want?'

'I believe you visited your wife in Colchester yesterday evening.'

'Wait till I finish this.'

Smedley restarted the saw and continued guiding the plank along the steel bench, cutting it in two lengthways. Switching off again, he lifted the heavy timbers as though they were weightless and laid them on the floor.

He wiped his hands on the apron then lifted the skirt to reach into a trouser pocket. Underneath the apron his flies gaped open. He pulled out a handkerchief and dropped the apron again.

'Yeah, I saw Rene last night,' he said, wiping his nose. 'So what?' The powerful hands mashed the handkerchief into a ball and returned it to the pocket. 'Made a complaint about it, has she?'

'No, though I understand you had words.'

The thick eyebrows came together in a continuous line across his forehead. 'Might've done.'

'D'you mind telling me what about?' Scobie took out his notebook.

'What's it to you, if Rene ain't complained?'

'We're investigating the death of the man in the flat above your wife's.'

The small eyes in the moon-shaped face grew smaller,

17

became black dots in white flesh. 'Dennison? That little tosser?'

'You knew him?'

'Yeah, I knew him. Kept sniffing round my Rene. Snuffed it, has he? Car accident?'

'No. He was murdered.'

Scobie watched Smedley's face for his reaction. There wasn't any . . . no surprise, no shock, no emotion of any kind.

'So . . . what d'you want with me then?' Smedley asked.

'A neighbour said you and your wife were quarrelling downstairs not long before Dennison came in last night. What was the row about?'

Smedley's massive shoulders rose and fell. 'I doesn't like Rene putting herself about so much. She's still my wife even if we's separated.'

'Apparently you objected to her going out with other men. Or is there one in particular you had in mind?'

Smedley half closed his eyes and looked away. 'Nah, no one special. It were more about her . . . tarting herself up. Asking for it, that's what she's bin doing. I won't have that.'

'What time did you leave?'

''Bout ten . . . mebbe a bit earlier.'

'And then what?'

'Drove home and went to bed.'

'What make of car d'you drive?'

'Ain't a car, it's a van, a blue Toyota.' Smedley watched Scobie writing the details in his notebook. 'Why you asking all these questions?'

'We have to account for everyone in the vicinity of the flat last night. You say you came back here and went to bed. Can anyone verify that?'

Smedley stared down at the floor. 'Nah, I live on me own.'

'Did you speak to Dennison on the phone last night?'

'Me?' His eyes narrowed. 'Why would I do that?'

'To warn him off your wife, perhaps,' Scobie suggested.

'Well, I didn't,' Smedley growled.

Scobie shut his notebook and returned it to his pocket. 'Thank you, Mr Smedley. I won't take any more of your time.'

'That it, then?' Smedley looked relieved.

'Yes, that's all for the moment.'

Scobie negotiated the obstacle course to the door and retraced his steps past the cottage and along the track to his car.

Bert Smedley was certainly capable of killing a man with his bare hands, Scobie thought as he drove through Sudbury on his way back to Colchester. John Dennison would have been a baby in those huge paws. And Smedley had no alibi for last night.

John Dennison's father and mother arrived from Eastbourne in the early afternoon. Millson took them in his car to the mortuary and the father formally identified his son's body.

Afterwards, Millson asked the questions he had to ask as gently as he could. No, their son had no enemies, they told him. Everyone liked him and there were no problems in his life they were aware of. They were stunned and mystified by his murder and had no idea what his killer might have been searching for in the flat.

His father had had the forethought to bring a recent photograph of Dennison. Millson sent it to be copied and duplicated for distribution to his officers and the media.

The autopsy began at three o'clock. The pyjama-clad body had already been photographed and labelled and the fingerprints taken. The pyjamas were now removed and examined for hairs, fibres, and stains and put into a plastic bag and labelled.

The naked body was weighed and specimens of hair taken from the head, eyebrows and pubis. The mouth and anus were swabbed and scrapings taken from the fingernails.

Millson waited outside the dissecting room until these routine procedures were over and joined David Duvall when he began his external examination of John Dennison's body.

The pathologist pointed to dark blue marks on the throat. 'Bruises don't show up for a time after death. The longer the time, the darker they get. Those marks are the result of pressure being applied to the throat, probably by thumbs compressing the windpipe. People can suffocate themselves and they can, and do, cut their own throats. What they can't do – at least, no one's managed it yet – is throttle themselves. I'm now going to remove the hyoid bone and see what that tells us.'

Millson turned his head away as Duvall made swift, decisive strokes with the scalpel.

'Hah!' Duvall laid the horseshoe-shaped bone on the dissecting table. 'It's fractured.' He turned to Millson. 'He was strangled as well as suffocated. I'd say his murderer pulled the plastic bag over his head, grabbed him round the neck to hold it in place, and dug his thumbs into his windpipe at the same time. Poor devil didn't stand a chance.'

While Millson was away an incident room had been set up at Colchester police station and equipped with filing cabinets, telephones and computer terminals. When he looked in after the postmortem, DCs were busy ringing the telephone numbers in John Dennison's address book. He saw Scobie was seated at a computer terminal and walked over to him.

'What did Mrs Smedley's husband have to say for himself, Norris?'

Scobie looked up from the keyboard. 'According to him the quarrel wasn't over a man, it was over the provocative way she dresses. She's right about him . . . he thinks he owns her. He says he drove straight home afterwards and went to bed. He lives alone, so there's no one to vouch for that.'

'Did he know Dennison?'

'Yes. He didn't like him. Reckoned he was hankering after his wife.'

'More like the other way round, I should think,' Millson said. 'Is he the type to do something about it?'

'Oh, definitely. He's an ugly character . . . and built like a tank. He'd wring Dennison's neck like a chicken's, if he'd a mind to.' Scobie turned round to the screen. 'I think he might have form so I've logged in to PNC criminal records.' He pressed a key. 'Here we are.' He leaned forward, studying the text. 'Thought so, two convictions for GBH.'

Millson rubbed his chin. 'I wonder if it was him Dennison was arguing with on the phone.'

'I asked him that. He denied it.'

'Get on to BT. They should be able to provide an itemized billing of Dennison's calls. If Dennison made the call and it lasted long enough, it'll tell us what number he was speaking to last night.' Millson leaned against the table and took out his cigarettes. 'Anything else come up while I was at the PM?'

'The scene of crime boys say the catch was forced on a downstairs sash window. No fingerprints, though, except Irene Smedley's, so presumably the intruder wore gloves. And they found fibres on the bedclothes which forensic are analysing.'

'What about the bag over his head?'

'Several prints on that. They're checking the national collection for a match. They won't find the killer's on it if he was wearing gloves, but there's a chance someone who handled it might have a record.'

'We need to trace that bag, if we can,' Millson said. 'I don't imagine the killer found it lying around handy in the flat. He brought it with him, so this is a premeditated murder and we can rule out an ordinary burglar who panicked. Send a team round the stores and electrical shops in the town with copies of the photograph. With luck, the bag is used to package one particular line of goods and we may be able to trace the purchasers.'

Late that afternoon, Millson released John Dennison's picture and personal details to the media with a brief statement that he had been suffocated and strangled. He appealed for anyone with information about the dead man, or who had seen him or spoken to him between nine o'clock and ten yesterday evening, to come forward.

The first response came next morning.

CHAPTER 3

Gary Saunders' black anorak was smothered with badges and chevrons and he wore his baseball cap back to front. A WPC escorted him to Millson's room and stood waiting by the door to escort him away again when he'd said his piece.

Gary delivered his information in bursts punctuated at frequent intervals with 'Know what I mean?' as though to give his brain time to catch up with his mouth. After the first few bursts Millson gave up trying to follow what he was saying and concentrated on distilling the essential facts from it.

When the flow ended, he said, 'So . . . you saw this man in the Oak Tree pub at Great Horkesley last night. Right?'

'Yeah, right. And—'

'Time?' Millson barked.

'Ah . . . time . . .' A problem for Gary, it seemed. 'Well . . . it were 'fore me mate come in at ten.'

'How long before? Five minutes? Half an hour?'

''Bout a quarter-hour.'

'What made you notice the man?'

'There was these two birds gabbing by the phone, see? Sharp dressers, and I had me eye on one of 'em, know what I mean? Then this guy goes to the phone an' blocks me view.'

Millson summarized: 'You saw this man using the phone at about a quarter to ten.'

'Right on,' said Gary.

'Did you notice him at any other time?'

23

Gary's brows twisted fiercely in thought. 'Nope,' he said. 'Don't think so 'cos I started eyeballing this bird, know what I mean? An'—'

'Thank you, Gary,' said Millson. 'Thank you for your help.'

'Yeah, right.' Gary came to his feet and looked around him. 'That all then?'

Millson paused in lighting a cigarette. Did he expect a reward or something?

'Doncha want me to write nuffing down?' Gary wanted to tell his mates he'd given the police a statement. And it might get on telly.

'No, that won't be necessary,' Millson said.

'Oh . . . right then.' A disappointed Gary shuffled from the room.

Millson gazed after him and wondered if he should be thankful Dena had brought home a Julie and not a Gary. He finished lighting his cigarette and summoned Scobie to his room by banging on the partition between their adjoining rooms.

'Dennison was seen drinking in the Oak Tree pub in Great Horkesley last night,' Millson told him. 'Tell press liaison to put out an appeal for anyone in the pub yesterday evening to contact the incident room. How far is it to Great Horkesley from his flat?'

'Five or six miles.'

'Say ten minutes' drive. If he drove straight there and straight back he'd be in the pub for about three-quarters of an hour. Trot along there with his picture and see if the staff remember him. The witness says he made a phone call from the bar around 9.45.'

'OK. No luck on the phone call from his flat, by the way. BT can't itemize calls in this area until the new exchange is in operation in December.'

'Damn!' Millson made a face.

'Some more information on Albert Smedley, though. I asked them to fax extracts from his case file. The GBH convictions were for beating up his wife's lovers – or at

24

least that's who he said they were. He got three months on the first occasion and six on the second.'

'H'm.' Millson stroked his chin. 'So he'd be likely to have a go at Dennison if he suspected any funny business between him and his wife.'

'And from what he told me, he did,' Scobie said.

'His wife said he was with her until about ten that night, though.'

'He could have come back later.'

'It's a thought,' said Millson.

Scobie returned from the Oak Tree after lunch. The bar had been crowded yesterday evening, but the barman remembered serving Dennison.

'He ordered a pint of lager,' Scobie told Millson, 'and that's all the barman saw of him. He says Dennison wasn't a regular . . . doesn't remember seeing him before.'

There were more responses over the following two days from people who had been in the Oak Tree the evening before the murder. As their reports were cross-referenced and checked against each other, the information hardened. John Dennison had sat in a window seat, drinking alone from soon after nine until a quarter to ten. At which time he'd rung a number on the payphone, apparently obtained no reply, and left.

'He drives to the pub, orders one drink, waits for over half an hour, tries the phone and drives home again,' Millson said. 'It doesn't take a genius to work out he went there to meet someone and they didn't show. Question is, who?'

'The same person he was arguing with on his phone at home?' Scobie suggested.

Millson nodded. 'Who might well be his killer.'

The detectives calling on stores and shops in the town with photographs of the plastic bag soon established that the bag was used to package a make of electric kettle. In response to a phone call, the manufacturer provided a list of retail outlets. Millson then redeployed his men over an area covering a thirty-mile radius from Colchester, to identify recent purchases of the kettle.

The particular kettle was an expensive, top-of-the-range model and Millson expected the number of sales to be relatively small.

Four days after the murder Millson received the forensic report on the fibres found on John Dennison's bedclothes. They were strands of blue serge and they matched none of Dennison's clothes in the flat. Their location on the bed suggested the killer had knelt astride his victim while he was strangling him and the fibres had come from his trousers.

Later the same day the full report of the postmortem arrived. Duvall had narrowed the time of death to between midnight and 3.00 a.m. and added an unexpected piece of information. The blood alcohol level of the dead man indicated consumption of a considerable amount of alcohol shortly before death.

Millson read the paragraph twice then rang the pathologist. 'These figures – percentages and blood alcohol ratios – they don't mean a damn thing to me. How much had he actually drunk?'

'The equivalent of half a bottle of whisky.'

'There can't be any doubt, I suppose?'

Duvall snorted down the phone. 'Not unless he could perform miracles and turn his blood to wine.'

'Thanks.'

Millson went next door to Scobie. 'The pathologist says Dennison was full of booze when he died. He didn't get that way on a pint of lager. Did you notice any drink in the flat?'

Scobie shook his head. 'Not even an empty bottle.'

'Neither did I. Come on' – Millson reached for his coat – 'I think Irene Smedley has been leading us up the garden.'

*　　　*　　　*

26

Irene Smedley welcomed them with a smile and led them into the kitchen. 'Don't mind if I carry on with me ironing, do you?' She fed the skirt of a print dress over the ironing board and lifted the iron from its stand. 'What can I do for you, gentlemen?' she asked cheerfully.

Her smile died as Millson said in a formal tone, 'Mrs Smedley, as the result of some information I've received I must ask you to elaborate on your relationship with the dead man.'

She replaced the iron and clasped her shoulders with her hands. 'Gives me the shivers hearing you call him the dead man. He was such a lively boy.' Her arms dropped. 'Let's go and sit in the lounge.'

They followed her past the open door of a bedroom to a bay-windowed room at the front of the house. Scobie glanced into the bedroom as he passed. There were gold-coloured silk sheets on the king-sized bed.

When they were seated, Irene Smedley asked cautiously, 'What d'you mean, elaborate on my relationship?'

'You told us Mr Dennison came in about ten the night he was murdered,' Millson said, 'and you heard him arguing on the phone soon after.'

'Ye-es.'

'And then you had a few stiff drinks and went to bed . . . "stoned", I think you said.'

'That's right.' She looked anxiously at Scobie as he took out a notebook.

'What did Mr Dennison do after his phone call?' Scobie asked.

Her face was tense. 'How should I know? Went to bed, I suppose. Like I told you, I was pissed. I didn't hear a thing.'

Millson said, 'You also told us he came down for a drink occasionally. Did he come down for one that night?'

'No!'

Millson rose from his chair and crossed to the cocktail cabinet. Casually, he picked up a bottle of vodka and put it down again, then did the same with a gin bottle and a whisky bottle.

Irene Smedley watched him nervously, her fingers twitching the hem of her red, pleated skirt.

'So how,' Millson asked, continuing to fiddle with other bottles, 'did he come to be as full of booze as a Scotsman at Hogmanay?'

She shrugged. 'How should I know? He'd been out to a pub, I suppose.'

Millson turned to her angrily. 'Don't fence with me, Mrs Smedley. We know that he only had one drink while he was out. And there's no drink in his flat – not so much as a can of beer. Now . . . the truth, please. He was down here drinking with you that night, wasn't he?'

Her shoulders drooped and she looked down at the floor. 'Yes.'

Millson returned to his seat. 'I want the whole story. Everything that happened after he returned here.'

She looked up. 'Story? There's no story. Johnny came down about half an hour after he got back. I'd . . . well, I'd sort of given him the come-on when he went out, so I weren't all that surprised to see him. We started drinking and after a while we . . . well, you know . . .'

'No, I don't know,' Millson said curtly.

The carmined lips curved. 'I took him to bed. You don't want the details, do you? We had drinks . . . went to bed . . . had more drinks . . . and later he went back upstairs. That's all I know. I didn't tell you before because . . .' She stopped and looked away from him. 'You said he was killed in the early hours of the morning. Well, he didn't leave me until after one and it's creepy having a guy turn into a corpse right after you've been bonking him. It made me feel very peculiar.' She shuddered and put her arms round her shoulders.

Scobie finished writing and looked up. In a businesslike tone of voice he said, 'Right, so we've established you had a sexual relationship with Mr Dennison and—'

'Hang on,' she said. 'Who said anything about a

28

relationship? That was the one and only time. Honest.' She saw the sceptical expression on their faces and said defiantly, 'OK, so I tried to get him into bed several times before. But that was the first time I managed it. And . . .' Her voice faltered. Suddenly her face puckered and tears squeezed out through the mascara. 'The silly bugger goes back to his own bed and gets murdered.'

Millson scrutinized her. The distress seemed genuine. He waited while she wiped her eyes with the back of her hand, then asked, 'While he was with you, did Mr Dennison say anything about where he'd been that evening, or who he went to meet?'

'No, nothing.' She tried to smile through the tears. 'We spent most of the time making love.'

'The row with your husband earlier in the evening,' Millson said, 'did Mr Dennison's name come up?'

She hesitated. 'Ye-es. But so did a dozen others. Bert thinks I have it off with every man I meet.'

She studied their faces. 'Look . . . God knows, I don't have any feelings for Bert, but you can't think he killed Johnny. He'd no reason to. He didn't know Johnny was here that night.'

Millson went to the window and looked out. 'What if he came back later? When you were . . .' He turned and waved a hand in the direction of the bedroom.

'Oh, God, no!' Her hand flew to her mouth.

'Then waited until Dennison returned upstairs and paid him a visit.'

'*No*!' Her voice went up an octave. 'Bert wouldn't do a thing like that.'

'Wouldn't he?' Scobie asked, opening his briefcase and taking out a typewritten sheet. 'He didn't exactly shake hands with the other men you had affairs with.' He began reading: 'Severe bruising . . . broken nose . . . concussion . . .'

'OK, Bert beat them up. But he wouldn't *kill* anyone,' she said.

29

Millson left the window and sat down again. 'Has your husband spoken to you since the murder?'

'He phoned me, yeah.'

'What did he want?'

She looked from one to the other.

'What did he want?' Millson repeated.

'He told me to button my lip about the row we had. Said it wouldn't look good with his record. That's all. Honest, that's all he said. And he's right. You're trying to stitch him up.'

'We're trying to establish the truth,' Millson said severely. 'One further question. Did you touch anything in Mr Dennison's flat after you discovered his body?'

'No.' She looked surprised.

'You didn't search through the drawers? Looking for love letters perhaps?'

'*Love* letters?' she asked incredulously. 'I'm not some lovesick teenager, I don't write my lovers no letters. No, 'course I didn't.'

'It was easy to kill Dennison,' said Millson as they drove away. 'He was drunk and Irene Smedley was out cold down below and couldn't hear anything.'

'If it was the husband, though, why search the flat?'

'Same reason as she might have had. To make sure there weren't any letters or notes from his wife lying around to incriminate him. I know she didn't write any, but he wasn't to know that.'

'I can see Smedley clamping his great paws round Dennison's neck and squeezing the life out of him for sleeping with his wife,' Scobie said, 'but why bother with that plastic bag?'

'So's his wife wouldn't hear the noise. He didn't know she was blotto.'

Scobie looked doubtful. 'Seems too calculated. I don't think that's Smedley's style.'

*   *   *

30

Thirty-five people had come forward in answer to the police appeal about the Oak Tree pub. The information they gave was recorded and cross-referenced in a computer file and the data was then analysed. It became clear from the descriptions and part descriptions given that a number of people in the bar had not come forward. Similarly, some of the vehicles in the car park were also unaccounted for.

Millson was not concerned. There were always people who missed appeals, or didn't respond for one reason or another, and he had all the information he needed from the Oak Tree for the present. The descriptions of the missing people and vehicles were printed out and put into a suspense file.

Two days later, Irene Smedley's other neighbours returned from holiday. As soon as the wife heard of the murder she picked up the phone and rang the police.

CHAPTER 4

Mr and Mrs Potter's house was separated from Irene Smedley's by a shared drive. They had been on a one-week holiday in Majorca and hadn't read any English newspapers while they were away.

'We never do on holiday,' Mrs Potter told Millson. 'We like to get away from everything and have a rest from all the bad news. I was dumbfounded when I heard about the murder next door.'

The previous Thursday, the night John Dennison was killed, they had been packing their suitcases before driving to Stansted to take an early morning flight. While Mrs Potter was hunting for her swimming costume in an upstairs room, she happened to look out of the window.

'I saw *him*,' she said. 'Bert Smedley – Irene's old man. He was in her garden. I didn't think much about it at the time because he's often round there pestering her.'

'You're sure it was him?' Millson asked.

'Oh, quite sure. There was a light on in Irene's flat and I saw his face as clear as anything.'

'What was he doing?'

'Leaning against the wall. Drunk, if you ask me.' Mrs Potter's mouth turned down at the corners. 'He was always coming home drunk when he lived there.'

'What time was this?'

'Getting on for one o'clock,' she said. 'I was keeping an eye on the time because we had to leave sharp at three to be at the airport in time to book in.'

'Did your husband see him too?'

'No, he was in the bathroom shaving. Vic shaves the

night before when we have an early flight. He likes to arrive at the hotel looking smart.'

'So, how long did you watch Mr Smedley for?'

'Oh, I didn't. I got on with our packing. As I said, I wasn't bothered because I've seen him calling on her at all hours. But as soon as I heard about the murder and the police were asking for information, I phoned the police station.'

Millson thanked her for coming and escorted her to an interview room for a WPC to take a written statement from her. Then he dispatched Scobie and a DC to bring Albert Smedley in for questioning. Smedley had motive, he'd been at the house at the time of the murder and he'd lied about his movements that night.

Albert Smedley had not come willingly. 'Why should I?' he growled when Scobie asked him to accompany him to the police station to assist with their inquiries. 'I've answered questions once.'

'You can come of your own accord or I can arrest you,' Scobie said.

'Yeah?' Smedley sneered. 'On what charge?'

'Obstructing police inquiries for a start. I wouldn't argue if I were you, Smedley. Not with your record.'

Smedley half closed his eyes slanting them to one side. The DC with Scobie took a step forward, expecting trouble. Smedley opened his eyes wide again and glared at him. 'Trust you lot to dig that up,' he said in a surly tone. 'All right, I'll come. I'll have to lock up first.'

The DC followed close behind as he went round the machines flicking off switches.

'Cost me a morning's work, this will,' Smedley grumbled as he entered the car.

In the interview room Smedley's hostility faded when Millson entered and lowered his bulk onto the chair next to Scobie. It was a reaction Scobie often noticed in suspects when they came face-to-face with Millson for the first time. Scobie was used to the close-cropped hair, the ape-length arms and the forbidding expression and knew that George Millson wasn't as hard as he looked. Smedley didn't know that, though, and he eyed Millson warily.

He listened attentively as Millson ran through the account he'd given Scobie of his movements on the night of the murder.

'And you didn't go out again? Looking for company, perhaps?' Millson asked in a friendly tone.

Smedley relaxed and gave a sly smile. 'Nah. Not much crumpet round where I live.'

'You're lying!' Smedley jumped at Millson's sudden bellow. 'You were seen in your wife's garden at one o'clock that night.'

Smedley's mouth opened and he bent forward as though he'd been punched in the stomach. His eyes went from side to side, avoiding Millson's.

'Anything you'd like to tell us?' Millson asked.

Smedley's restless eyes fastened on Scobie opening a notebook. 'I ain't saying nothing.'

Millson sighed. 'We know you went back there, so you might as well admit it.' As Smedley's mouth set obstinately, he said sharply, 'Dennison was your wife's lover and you make a habit of beating up her lovers. What happened this time? You lost control and went too far?'

When Smedley stayed silent Millson went on, 'He was screwing her that evening . . .' He saw Smedley's eyes blaze with anger. 'Screwing her,' he repeated with emphasis, 'and it sent you wild. So, when he was upstairs asleep, you broke in and strangled him because you couldn't stand your wife having it off with a young—'

'Shut yer filthy mouth about Rene!' Smedley burst out. 'An' stop winding me up. I didn't do nothing like that.'

'So, what *did* you do?'

Smedley's face was immobile, but he'd begun to sweat and drops of perspiration showed in the wrinkles in his forehead.

Millson's tone became friendly again. 'It was Mrs Potter, you know, who saw you at your wife's house.'

Smedley stirred in his seat. ' 'T'ain't Rene's house. It's half mine and I've a right to be there.'

'Fair point,' Millson said amicably. 'So, you admit you were there. What were you doing?'

'Keeping an eye on Rene.'

'At one o'clock in the morning?' Scobie asked.

Smedley's eyes wandered away to a corner of the room. 'She were all tarted up when I called earlier, so I knew she'd got the hots for someone. I went back to find out who.'

'And do what?' Millson asked.

'Beat hell outta him when he left!' Smedley said savagely, bunching his fists. 'They don't hang round Rene no more when I've finished with 'em.'

'I can understand how you feel,' Millson said in a sympathetic voice to encourage Smedley to keep talking. 'What time would this be?'

'Dunno. I was a bit pissed, see? I'd been boozing in the Albert for a coupla hours. 'Bout half twelve, I reckon. The lights was on in the front room. I peeped in an' couldn't see no one so I goes round the back. Rene's bedroom light was on. I hung around waiting for him to come out the front door. Then I heard her door open and close an' I see'd Dennison's lights upstairs come on. So I knew it was him she'd been setting her cap at. But I couldn't do nothing 'bout it then. So I left.'

'What time?'

'I dunno. Must've bin after one, I suppose.'

'The trouble is, you see,' Millson said in a patient tone, 'there's no one to say when you left.'

'Why would I hang about?' Smedley asked. 'I'll admit I'd have crippled the little sod if I could've got hold of him, but I couldn't.'

'Why not? What was to stop you beating up Dennison there and then? You know the house, you'd have no trouble getting in.'

'Yeah, but I couldn't have him hollering and screaming

with Rene downstairs. She'd be straight on the blower to you lot. I was gonna see to him later.'

'I don't believe you,' Millson said. 'Oh, you were afraid he'd make a noise, all right. That's why you put a bag over his head when you killed him. You broke in through the hall window—'

'I didn't! I went home like I said. Yeah, I thought about busting in, but I'd have bin seen 'cos there was a guy sitting in a car watching.'

'Oh, yes? Just remembered this, have you?' Millson asked sarcastically.

'He was there, I tell you. The other side of the road. Mebbe he was casing the houses, or checking on his missus like me. I dunno. But he was there an' he see'd me.'

'Describe him,' Scobie said.

'Couldn't see his face in the dark, could I?'

'Can't describe the car either, I suppose?'

'Yeah, I can. It were a Volvo Estate,' Smedley said confidently. 'Light colour – silver or grey, p'raps.'

Millson gave a sigh. 'Not exactly uncommon, are they?' he said sceptically. 'Let's turn to something else. The Oak Tree pub at Great Horkesley.'

'Never heard of it,' Smedley said.

'You arranged to meet Dennison there and didn't show up because you were engaged in a violent quarrel with your wife.'

'I said I don't know it.'

'And later he phoned you to find out why, and you had an argument.'

'What yer saying is all cock to me,' Smedley said. 'Flippin' rubbish.'

The questioning continued for a while with Millson and Scobie putting the questions alternately. Smedley stuck to his story.

At the end, Millson stood up and said wearily, 'All right, Smedley. Sergeant Scobie will have a statement typed out for you to sign and then he'll take you back.'

Outside the interview room he said to Scobie, 'Have a look round while you're there. See if he's got one of those electric kettles or a pair of blue serge trousers. And it's probably a waste of time, but we'll have to look into his story about the man in a Volvo. Add an appeal for him to the next press release and put a couple of DCs onto calling at the houses around Dennison's to ask if anyone else saw this man.'

A week later Millson began to feel uneasy about the case. Scobie had found no further evidence at Smedley's cottage and the inquiries about the man in the Volvo were inconclusive. Two people thought they'd seen a man sitting in a car about that time, though they were not sure of the make or exactly where in the street it had been parked. And the detectives tracing purchasers of the electric kettle had interviewed a number of people without result.

In the hope of finding a new lead, Millson decided to launch an appeal for the missing witnesses from the Oak Tree pub.

Before then, the incident room had a visitor. He asked for the keys to John Dennison's flat and a DC brought him smartly to Millson.

Ken Clark was a red-haired young man in thick-lensed spectacles that magnified his eyes and gave him an owlish appearance. He wore an ill-fitting blue suit, and the knot of his red tie hung loosely.

'The department has sent me down to retrieve an official file Mr Dennison had on loan, Chief Inspector,' he explained. 'Your officers say it's not among his effects and it isn't in his flat. I – I thought I might look for myself . . . er – here's my official pass.' He scrabbled in a pocket and pulled out a card-holder.

Millson waved it aside. 'What sort of file?'

'One of our personnel files.'

'What's in it?'

'Mostly correspondence with staff who worked for the department a long time ago.'

'Why should Mr Dennison have a file like that in his flat?'

'There was a reunion last November . . . staff who were evacuated to Bournemouth fifty years ago. John had the job of tracing them. He took the file home to work on because he was arranging another get-together next year. And now he's . . . um . . . gone . . . I've taken over his work and I'm a bit lost without the file. Are you sure your men didn't find it? Lock it away for safety, perhaps?' he asked hopefully.

'I'm sure,' Millson said flatly. The forensic and scene of crime teams who had scoured the flat for minute fibres of cloth and other clues would hardly have overlooked an official file, or omitted to log it if they'd taken it. 'Is that all it contains? Correspondence about a reunion?'

'Yes, except . . .' Clark hesitated. 'Well, John did make a lot of notes, so they'd be in the file too.'

'Notes about what?'

'Things people told him about themselves. John was good at getting people to talk. He spent nine months tracing these evacuees, visiting addresses and so on. Some of the things he heard were pretty hair-raising, apparently. He was going to refer to one or two in his speech at the reunion, but he got cold feet.'

Millson leaned back in his chair and contemplated the wall of his office beyond Clark's head. His thoughts on the case began travelling a new path. Ken Clark, thinking he was the object of the chief inspector's attention, shifted uncomfortably in his seat.

After a moment or two Millson said, 'The names and addresses of these people, d'you have a note of them somewhere, Mr Clark?'

'Only of the ones who were invited to the reunion. They were made honorary members of HORSA – the Home Office Retired Staff Association – so the information will be in our membership records.'

38

'I want their names and addresses as quickly as possible,' Millson said crisply.

Ken Clark looked startled. 'Do you think the file is connected with John's murder, then?'

'If his killer took it, it is,' Millson said grimly.

'The most likely reason for the murderer to take that file,' Millson said, as he told Scobie of Clark's visit, 'is that it contains information about him he doesn't want known.'

'You're thinking of blackmail? Dennison was blackmailing someone?'

'I think it's possible. What do we know about his finances?'

Scobie half closed his eyes in concentration. 'Comfortable bank balance . . . about five thousand in savings . . .' His eyes opened again. 'And he owned a very expensive car – a Lotus Esprit. It was in Mrs Smedley's garage.'

'Nice going for a junior civil servant,' Millson commented. He thought for a while. 'It's time we paid his girlfriend, Sarah Howarth, a visit. She's kept a remarkably low profile since the day of the murder. Let's see what she can tell us about him.'

Sarah Howarth's flat in Ipswich was simple and functional. Totally impersonal, Scobie thought, glancing around as they entered. It gave no clue to the character – or even the sex – of the person living there. There were no personal belongings lying around, no knick-knacks, none of the feminine touches that adorned Kathy Benson's flat.

It was early evening and Sarah Howarth was still wearing her office clothes, a black barathea suit and white shirt with pearl buttons. Her eyes were cool and expressionless as Millson began by asking her how long she'd known John Dennison.

'Three months. We met in January.'

'Do you know the Oak Tree pub at Great Horkesley?'

'Only from seeing your appeal on television. I've never been there.'

'We now know that Mr Dennison was there the evening before he was murdered, and that he hadn't been seen in the pub before. Do you have any idea why he went there?'

She shook her head. 'No. As I said before, the last time I spoke to him was at the theatre two nights earlier.'

'Witnesses say he appeared to be waiting for someone. Do you know who that might have been?'

'No.'

'Some witnesses have also said he tried to telephone someone . . . at about a quarter to ten. Were you at home then?'

She hesitated. 'Er . . . probably not. I didn't feel well that evening and I went out to get some medicine from a late-night chemist's.'

'What was Mr Dennison like with money?' Millson asked. 'Was he free with it, would you say?'

She frowned. 'What a strange question.' She shrugged. 'He certainly wasn't mean.'

Scobie said, 'He seems to have had plenty, and he drove a Lotus Esprit. That was a bit expensive for someone on his salary, wasn't it?'

She raised one eyebrow at him. 'I don't know. I'm not in the habit of asking my boyfriends how much they earn.'

Millson grunted and asked, 'Did he talk to you about his work?'

Her shoulders rose and fell. 'Not really. I knew he was the secretary of some retired staff association, but that's about all.'

'You've been to his flat, I imagine?'

'A few times . . . for coffee.'

'Apparently, he took some of his work home. Did you notice any papers – or a file – lying around?'

'Not that I remember.' Her mouth curved in a smile. 'John's place was always a tip. Why? Is something missing?'

'Yes. An official file of names and addresses.'

Her eyes flickered. 'I didn't see anything like that,' she said. The eyes were steady again.

*   *   *

After they left, Sarah Howarth poured herself a large vodka and added a dash of orange. She took a small sip and rubbed her lips together, savouring the taste. Curling herself into an armchair, she tucked her feet beneath her and sat holding the glass and gazing into space.

She hadn't expected to be questioned like that. Hadn't expected to be questioned at all, in fact. She took another sip of her drink. Still, she'd come through it all right. No slip-ups.

She stretched languidly and rested her head against the armchair. Raising the glass to her lips, she tipped her head back and let the spirit trickle slowly into her mouth.

CHAPTER 5

Ken Clark faxed the names and addresses to Millson the next day. There were forty-five names and the addresses were spread around the country, although most of them were in the south-east.

In an accompanying note Clark explained that two hundred staff had been evacuated to Bournemouth in 1940. Twenty-five were killed in the war – including two girls killed in the hit-and-run raids on the town which began soon after they arrived. Fifty-nine had died in the post-war years and seventy-one hadn't been traced. Many of these were girls who'd left the department on marriage or not returned to it after the war. Forty-five of the original two hundred evacuees had been traced. Twenty-six had attended the reunion on the fiftieth anniversary in 1990 and three had died since.

Millson had copies made of the names and addresses and called his team together for a briefing. He told them he now suspected John Dennison had been blackmailing.

'If I'm right, that person may be on this list,' he said, 'and I don't want him – or her – alerted. So, there's to be no mention of blackmail . . . just say we're speaking to all known contacts of the murdered man. Find out when they last heard from him or saw him, and where they were on the night of the murder. Then check it out. One other thing. These people were all invited to a reunion last November. The names of those who went are ticked. Ask the others why they didn't go.'

Later, a collator keyed the names into the computer case file. During the entry procedure a search program automatically scanned the database to see if any name had been mentioned before in the case. One name had and a warning flag appeared on the screen with a reference to its location in the data. The name, Abigail Labram, occurred in a statement made by a Mrs Penelope Troop.

The statement was drawn from the filing cabinet. Penelope Troop was one of the missing witnesses from the Oak Tree who had responded to Millson's further appeal the day before. In her statement she mentioned seeing several people she knew in the bar on the evening of the murder. One of them was Abigail Labram.

The coincidence was brought to Scobie's attention and he reported it to Millson.

'Abigail Labram's husband is on that list of names Clark gave us too,' he told Millson. 'And they live locally in Beaumont cum Moze. I wonder why neither of them came forward?'

'Probably missed the appeal,' Millson said. 'Surprising how many people do. They'll have to be checked. We'll do some legwork ourselves, Norris. Nothing's happening here and I need an excuse to get out of the office for a while.'

Scobie looked at his watch. It was nearly lunch time. He and Kathy had been awaiting a chance to tell George Millson they planned to set up home together. They were not sure how he would take it and Kathy was anxious for reassurance it would not affect Norris's promotion prospects.

'D'you think we could stop on the way for a beer and a sandwich in Tanniford?' he asked Millson.

'At the Black Dog, I presume?' Millson grinned. 'That's where Kathy lunches, isn't it?'

'Yes, and if it's all right with you, I'd like to ask her to join us. There's something she wants your advice about.'

'That's fine by me. Give her a ring. And tell her I'd like some advice about Dena in return.'

*   *   *

43

Over lunch, Scobie let Kathy do the talking. He knew George Millson had a soft spot for Kathy and he hoped those wide violet eyes of hers would do the rest and win Millson's support.

They did. In no time at all he heard Millson say cheerfully, 'No problem with that. It's about time you two got together. Let me know what you'd like for a house-warming present.'

'Thanks, we'll do that.' Kathy gave him a warm smile. 'What did you want to ask me about Dena?'

'Um . . . well . . .' said Millson, changing from policeman to baffled father.

Last Saturday, Dena had appeared mid-afternoon with her stiffly lacquered hair sticking up in spikes all over her head.

'She looked like a floating sea mine,' Millson said.

Kathy giggled. 'Is that what you told her?'

'No, she wouldn't understand about mines. I told her she looked like a hedgehog. She's hardly spoken to me since.'

'I'm not surprised,' Kathy said. 'Next time, try telling her she looks nice. You'll find that makes her much easier to manage.'

'Really?' Millson was unconvinced.

'She's looking for masculine attention and approval,' Kathy went on, 'and the worst thing you can do is to criticize her or put her down. Flatter her! Take it from me, it'll work.'

As they were leaving, Millson casually mentioned they were on their way to Beaumont cum Moze. 'Place called Spencers,' he told her.

Kathy's estate agency had been her father's before he retired and had handled many of the property sales in the area. Kathy had worked there since she left school and was a fund of information on local inhabitants.

'The Labrams live there,' she said. 'Charming couple. One of my first big sales. They retired there about ten years ago. Pots of money. The husband's an ex-airline pilot who started a small airline of his own. The story is he sold it for millions when he retired and bought Spencers.' Her lips parted in a smile. 'You were fishing, weren't you? Anything else you'd like to know?'

Millson returned her smile. 'Any scandal?'

'Not that I've heard.'

Spencers overlooked Landermere Creek at the end of Hamford Water. Driving in through the gates, Scobie had the sensation of entering a past era. March had given way to April and the carpets of daffodils beneath the trees were in full bloom. It was like watching a period drama on television as the title captions finished rolling.

The impression was reinforced by a maid in uniform. She asked their names as she opened the double doors of the large Edwardian house and bade them wait in the library. Scobie had the feeling that if he hadn't telephoned before he left the office to say they were coming, she would have turned them away and told them to make an appointment.

The maid reappeared and showed them into a spacious drawing room with long windows looking out on a formal garden. There was a boxed seat running along beneath the windows which had internal shutters folded back against the wall.

Abigail Labram and her husband and son were standing in a row with their backs to the white marble fireplace. They looked as though they were posing for a photograph, Scobie thought.

Abigail Labram was slim and had a small, childlike face that made her seem much younger than he knew her to be. She was wearing a charcoal-grey trouser suit. Her silver-grey hair, cut in a bob, shone evenly like polished steel.

Her husband, Michael, was tall. His fair hair was streaked with white and he wore brown corduroys and a hacking jacket.

The son, Edgar, whom Abigail introduced to them as a solicitor, was middle-aged. He wore a dark blue suit with a waistcoat and his hair was straw-coloured. 'Edgar lives with us,' she said. She didn't explain why he was present in the room, though, Scobie noticed.

'Please sit down.' Abigail Labram seated herself in a wing chair. It was one of a half-dozen armchairs arranged in a semi-circle around the fireplace. Millson and Scobie sat down opposite her. Her husband and son remained standing.

She spoke in a soft, quiet voice. 'I understand this is about the murder of poor Mr Dennison. Why have you come to us, Chief Inspector?'

Millson gave her the explanation he'd instructed his team to use. 'We're speaking to everyone he had contact with, Mrs Labram, and I understand you and your husband were invited to a reunion Mr Dennison organized last year.'

'Yes, he wrote to us about it and we spoke on the telephone once or twice. But that's all. We never actually met him.'

Her husband cleared his throat. 'I did,' he said. 'He called here one day last summer. You were out, Abby. He was gathering information about the evacuation in 1940 . . . trying to trace everyone.'

'Oh . . . I didn't know that,' she said.

'You didn't go to the reunion, though?' Scobie asked. Their names hadn't been ticked on Clark's list.

'No,' she said. 'Meeting people I hadn't seen for fifty years would have made me sad. We were all so very young then.'

Michael Labram added, 'We didn't return to the office after the war, you see. I went straight from the RAF to British Airways and Abby had a son to bring up.'

'And you didn't keep in touch with the others?' Millson asked.

'No, we didn't,' said Abigail Labram.

'Though you did hear from Midge a couple of weeks back,' her husband reminded her.

46

'Yes, but that was the first time in years,' she said quickly.

'Midge?' Millson asked.

'Marjorie Wilson,' she said. 'We shared a flat in Bournemouth during the war.'

Millson nodded and led her to the purpose of his visit. 'Do you know the Oak Tree pub in Great Horkesley, Mrs Labram?'

Her eyebrows lifted. 'No, I'm afraid I don't.'

'The reason I ask is that a woman said she saw you there the night Mr Dennison was murdered.'

'That's ridiculous! She must have mistaken someone else for me. Who was it?'

'A Mrs Penelope Troop.'

She shook her head. 'I don't know any Mrs Troop.'

'In her statement she says she recognized you from the yacht club at Walton.'

'Well, that explains it then,' she said confidently. 'My husband's the member, not me. I hardly ever go there.' She gave her husband an arch look. 'She's probably seen Michael with one of those yachtie wives who crew for him, and thought she was his wife. That's who she saw at the Oak Tree, not me.'

'I see,' said Millson. 'Just for the record then, perhaps you wouldn't mind telling me where you were that evening?'

'Not at all. I spent the evening with Charm.'

'Charm?' Scobie queried, looking up from his notes.

'*Charmian*,' Abigail Labram said impatiently. 'Charmian Carson. She's a friend of mine.'

Scobie nodded. 'May I have her address, please?'

'She lives at The Cedars. It's the other side of Wix.'

'Well, that seems to clear things up,' said Millson rising to his feet. 'I won't take up any more of your time. Thank you for your help.'

He was preoccupied as they drove out through the gates. 'Do you believe her?' Scobie asked.

Millson grunted. 'I'm not sure. There was something about her manner that wasn't right. She was on edge, I think. And why was that son there? For moral support? Or because he was a solicitor?'

'Yes, that did seem odd.'

'I suppose she could have had a date with someone that evening and didn't want her husband to know about it,' Millson mused.

'At her age?'

'Why not? She's still attractive,' Millson said. 'She must have been a very pretty girl.'

'Well, if you're thinking of her as Dennison's blackmail victim, I don't see the husband as his killer. He must be in his late sixties at least.'

'Since when has age been a barrier to committing murder?' Millson demanded. 'If you bothered to study the homicide statistics you'd know that half a dozen murders in the last three years were committed by men over sixty-five.'

'I don't expect they strangled fit young men, though,' Scobie retorted.

'No, Norris,' Millson said patiently, 'their victims were usually young children or older women. But Dennison was in a drunken sleep. And Michael Labram looked pretty fit to me.'

Chastened, Scobie asked, 'Shall I check Mrs Labram's alibi with her friend, Charmian, then?'

Millson shook his head. 'There's no point. She wouldn't have offered it if she hadn't made sure it would stand up.'

At home that evening, Millson gazed askance at his daughter's latest creation for a school disco. Her dark hair was shorter than usual and the ends were coloured green. She wore a black satin waistcoat and the green mini skirt barely covered the crutch of her black tights.

He took a deep breath and placed his trust in the advice Kathy Benson had given him at lunch time. Forcing his face into a smile he said, 'You look nice, Dena.'

48

Her head swung round, eyes narrowed in suspicion. 'What do you want? I'm *not* going to do the hoovering. It's your turn.'

His smile became genuine at her reaction. 'I don't want anything. I just think you look nice.'

'You do?' she asked unbelievingly. She twirled round, flaring the skirt. 'Really?'

'Really,' he lied. 'Only – um . . . what about school on Monday?'

'Oh, don't worry, it washes out,' she said. She leaned down and smoothed a wrinkle in her tights. 'Are you going to pick me up after?'

Millson relaxed. He'd been expecting a confrontation over bringing her straight home after the disco. 'Would you like me to?'

'Yes, please.' She stepped forward and kissed his cheek. It lasted longer than the usual peck.

CHAPTER 6

Marjorie Wilson unlocked the front door of her terrace house in Westcliff, stepped into the hall and took off her coat. Underneath she wore a white satin blouse and a brown, pleated skirt. Closing the door behind her she hung her coat on a peg and walked down the hall and into the kitchen. She picked up the electric kettle and turned to the sink to fill it. Suddenly she froze, her hand on the tap. *Someone was coming down her stairs.*

She lived alone in the house. She had been alone since Gerald died two years ago, the year he should have retired on a pension. Panic-stricken, Marjorie glanced towards the back door. It was locked and bolted and led only to an enclosed patio. Dropping the kettle with a clatter, she made a dash for the front door past the foot of the stairs.

He caught her as she was pulling open the door. Throwing an arm round her neck from behind, he choked off her scream and kicked the door shut with his foot. Then he dragged her down the hall to the kitchen and forced her into a chair.

Plucking a carving knife from the magnetic rack on the wall by the cooker he brandished it in front of her. 'Keep quiet or I'll stick this in you!'

She stared at him, terrified. He was wearing a suit with a collar and tie and apart from his black gloves, shiny and sinister, he didn't seem like a burglar. What was he, then? She kept her eyes off the gloves and fought down panic.

'What do you want? I don't have much money, but you can take all I've got. My bag—'

'Shut up!' Still holding the knife, he was searching the

kitchen drawers. He found the length of cord she used for a clothesline. Uncoiling it, he moved towards her.

'Please don't tie me up,' she begged.

Ignoring her, he tied her ankles to the chair legs, pulled her arms round the back of the chair and tied her hands together. He took a handkerchief from his pocket and stuffed it into her mouth, then secured it with a duster from the kitchen drawer, forcing it between her teeth and knotting it behind her head.

She was gripped by a feeling of dread as he stood back and surveyed her. If he did anything . . . touched her . . . she would go to pieces. Apparently satisfied, he put down the knife and went out into the hall. She heard him ascending the stairs.

She began struggling, flexing her wrists and ankles and trying to free herself. He'd tied her securely, though. Above her head there were occasional sounds of movement as if he were going from room to room.

After a while he came downstairs and went into the front room. Then she heard him in the small dining room, opening the drawers of her desk, rustling papers. Clearly he was searching. For what, though? Did he think she had money hidden somewhere? Surely he would have questioned her about it if he thought that?

Marjorie began to feel calmer. This had to be some dreadful mistake and he thought she was someone else. Either that, or he had the wrong address. Yes, that's what it had to be. He wasn't going to attack her and when he realized his mistake he would untie her and leave.

There was a long silence and she became unnerved. When he at last returned to the kitchen he was holding some sheets of paper in his hand. He thrust them down in front of her on the table. They were her bank statements.

'I knew it had to be you,' he said in an ugly tone.

She shook her head and tried to speak through the gag to tell him she didn't know what he meant.

'There!' He stabbed angrily at an entry with his finger. 'There's the proof.'

She looked down. It was a credit of five thousand pounds made to her account a month ago. Again she shook her head and tried to mouth sounds through the gag. If only he would remove it she could explain. Instead, he took a small notepad and a ballpoint pen from beside the telephone on the worktop and placed them in front of her. Stooping, he unfastened the clothesline from her wrists and ankles, picked up the knife and sat down on the other side of the table.

'Write!' he snarled.

She stared at the small pad of paper. How could she explain in a few written words on these four-inch squares of paper that she didn't know where the money had come from? That it had been deposited anonymously and that she'd asked the bank about it. All they could tell her was that the deposit had been made in cash at a branch in Tothill Street in London by, according to the paying-in slip, 'J. Smith'.

She didn't know any J. Smith, certainly not one who would give her five thousand pounds. She'd known a Bill Smith long, long ago – had been engaged to him, in fact. He'd been killed in the war, though.

She took up the pen and wrote: *I don't know where the money came from*, and pushed the pad across the table to him. He read it and tossed it back at her, his eyes flaring angrily.

'You're lying!'

She seized the pad, tore off the top note and wrote urgently: *I don't know what you mean. You're mistaking me for someone else.* She held the second note out to him.

He read it and started haranguing her, calling her names, making accusations that were meaningless to her and working himself into a rage. Somehow she had to make him understand, and that meant speaking. Also, she was afraid the sodden handkerchief in her mouth would slip down her throat and choke her. She'd read of victims dying accidentally like that.

She dropped the note, tore off another square of paper

and wrote: *It hurts. I can't stand it any longer*. She pointed her finger at the gag and pushed the note across to him. As he read it his expression changed.

'All right,' he said, 'stay there and don't move.' He waved the knife threateningly.

Gathering up the clothesline, he went out to the hall. Moments later he returned and unfastened her gag.

She dragged air into her lungs, sighing with relief. 'I can explain everything,' she began. 'I—'

'You can do your talking in the hall.' He pulled her from the chair and pushed her through the door.

In the hall, the small mahogany table that normally stood under a mirror by the front door had been moved into the corner of the stairwell outside the kitchen door. One of her dining-room chairs stood next to it.

'Get up and stand on the table,' he ordered.

Puzzled, she hesitated. He raised the knife. 'Do as you're told!'

She clutched the back of the chair and climbed awkwardly onto the table. He stepped up behind her and reached up to the banisters along the landing above. She glanced up and went rigid with shock. From between the banisters he was pulling down the clothesline. It had been tied round two of the banisters and there was a noose in the end of it. Before she could move he had dropped it over her head and pulled the noose taut.

'Stand still, or you'll hang yourself,' he warned.

He jumped down from the table, moved the chair away from it and sat down. 'Now you can talk,' he said, gazing up at her sardonically.

She began to speak rapidly, trying to convince him that she had no idea where the money had come from. Even to her ears the explanation sounded absurd. The harder she tried, the more he sneered at her, ridiculing her story. He asked her what she'd done with the money and she told him she'd used it to reduce her mortgage because she had very little income since Gerald died and was having great difficulty in making ends meet. He nodded, smiling knowingly, and she realized it was the wrong thing to have said.

Perhaps someone had swindled money from him and he thought it was her. As she was about to say it couldn't be her because she had no idea who he was, she looked down at him. Something about the sneering smile, the way the upper lip rose on one side and exposed his teeth, brought a sudden stab of memory. Another face had smiled like that. She stared down into the cold blue eyes.

'My God!' she breathed. 'I know who you are.'

His eyes flared with alarm and in a sudden movement he took hold of the table legs and yanked the table from under her.

Marjorie Wilson dropped, the noose jerked tight round her throat and she dangled, legs kicking wildly in a flurry of white petticoat.

The man watched her for a moment then returned to the kitchen and collected up the three notes she had written. He placed the one which read: *It hurts. I can't stand it any longer* in the middle of the kitchen table and put the other two in his pocket. Then he returned the bank statements to the bureau desk in the dining room and went round the house to make sure he'd left no traces of his visit.

Finally, back in the hall, he carefully positioned the mahogany table a foot away from Marjorie Wilson's now lifeless hanging body and let himself out of the front door.

The local police found no signs of a forced entry and no suspicious circumstances. They examined the simple knots securing the clothesline to the landing banisters and studied the position of the table in the hall. From this evidence, and the note on the kitchen table, they concluded that Marjorie Wilson had hanged herself by jumping off the hall table.

The subsequent postmortem and the evidence of a handwriting expert, who confirmed that Marjorie Wilson had written the note, provided further corroboration that she had hanged herself.

At the inquest a few days later the coroner asked Marjorie Wilson's GP a question: 'Can you throw any light on the note she left, doctor? What she might be referring to by: "It hurts. I can't stand it any longer"?'

'I think so. She and her partner had been together for many years and I gather she was extremely fond of him. When he died suddenly it was a terrible shock to her. She became very depressed and, in fact, I've been treating her for depression for some time. I imagine the note means the pain of losing him was too great to bear and she couldn't go on any longer.'

'Thank you, doctor.'

Dr Ponsonby hadn't finished, however. 'But I would have thought that if she wanted to take her own life, an overdose of the Valium tablets I prescribed would have been far less traumatic.'

The coroner had dealt with many cases of suicide and considered he knew a lot more than Dr Ponsonby about the methods people chose to end their lives. He dismissed the slight doubt the doctor had introduced into the proceedings.

'In my experience,' he said ponderously, 'people who are determined to take their own life don't give them-selves the chance to change their mind. Taking an over-dose leaves you the opportunity of making a 999 call at the last moment. Jumping off a table with a rope round your neck is irrevocable.'

The coroner recorded his verdict that Marjorie Wilson had taken her own life in a fit of depression following the death of her partner.

Two days later, the team of detectives who had been allot-ted T–Z of the names on Kenneth Clark's list to interview, reached W.

CHAPTER 7

Millson was frustrated by the lack of progress. Nearly all the people who had bought that type of electric kettle had been traced, interviewed and eliminated from the inquiry. Likewise, the teams working through Kenneth Clark's list had not turned up a likely murderer or blackmail victim, and everyone interviewed so far had given a satisfactory explanation of their whereabouts on the night of the murder.

'Anything new?' he asked hopefully when Scobie put his head round the door of his room.

'There's a nil result from one of the names Clark gave us. The lady is dead.'

Millson said gloomily, 'I expect one or two more will pop off before we reach the end of them.'

'This one didn't die of old age. She committed suicide.'

Millson's head reared up. 'Who was it?'

'Marjorie Wilson, the woman Mrs Labram said she'd just heard from again. She hanged herself last week. In Westcliff.'

Millson rubbed his chin. He badly needed a fresh lead, a new direction to follow. 'Ask the local police to fax us a copy of the reports on the case, Norris.'

Marjorie Wilson's suicide note bothered Millson. Scobie watched him frown over the fax copy, then pick it up and push it across his desk.

'What does that mean to you, Norris? "It hurts. I can't stand it any longer."'

'That she was suffering from some unbearably painful illness.'

'Not according to her doctor, she wasn't. He reckoned she killed herself because she was depressed over the death of her partner.'

'The note could mean that too, I suppose,' Scobie said.

'Not to me, it couldn't,' Millson said, 'but then I didn't know the lady. Find out when the funeral is. I'd like to learn more about her and see who turns up.'

Marjorie Wilson's only surviving relative was a nephew, Tony Brett, who was also the sole beneficiary under her will. He was disappointed to discover there was a large mortgage on her house and she had little in the way of savings.

He made arrangements for a modest funeral and phoned the handful of numbers in her address book to let people know of her death and the time and place of the funeral. He wasn't expecting more than one or two to attend and was pleasantly surprised on the day of the funeral to see a dozen or so people as he followed the coffin into the crematorium at Southend. It made his aunt's departure from the world seem less of a lonely one.

Millson and Scobie joined the mourners as they gathered in the gardens of the crematorium after the ceremony. Millson noticed Abigail Labram amongst them, standing with two other women. She was crying. She looked startled when she saw him and averted her head.

Scobie tapped his arm. 'Ken Clark's here too.'

Millson nodded. 'Yes, I suppose he attends all the funerals now he's taken over Dennison's job. Have a quiet word with him and find out which of these people here are on the list he sent us. I'll speak to the nephew.'

Millson introduced himself to Tony Brett and offered his condolences. Tony Brett looked worried. 'Mr Clark said you're investigating the murder of his predecessor, John Dennison. Is something wrong?'

'No, we're just here to clear up a loose end. My men

have been interviewing everyone who had contact with Mr Dennison and, unhappily, your aunt died before they were able to speak to her. I wonder if we might look through her correspondence to see if she had any letters from him?'

'Yes, OK. I'm going on to the house when this is over.'

'I was surprised to see Abigail Labram there,' Millson said as he followed Tony Brett's car out of the crematorium. 'She said she hadn't heard from Marjorie Wilson for years until her call a week or so ago. Who else on Clark's list turned up?'

Scobie flipped open his notebook. 'Four others. Peggy Barton, now Mrs Pennington . . . Rachel Green . . . David Nelson . . . Betty Foster, formerly Verrier. Clark says if we need any more information, the person to ask is Betty Foster. She kept up with a lot of the staff who were evacuated to Bournemouth and, in fact, provided Dennison with most of his information about them. Apparently, she continued working in the department after the war until she retired several years ago.'

In the hallway of Marjorie Wilson's house Millson gazed up at the landing banisters.

'She was found hanging from there,' her nephew said. 'Apparently, she tied her clothesline to the banisters then stood on the hall table, knotted it round her neck and jumped off.'

'Did your aunt ever mention suicide to you?' Millson asked.

'No, but then I hardly knew her. A card at Christmas was about the only communication we had with each other.'

'Uh-huh.' Millson nodded and walked through to the kitchen, peering around.

'Are you looking for something, Chief Inspector?'

'A notepad. About four inches square.'

'There's one by the phone.' Brett pointed.

Millson picked up the pad and examined it. The top sheet was blank. 'Have you used this at all, Mr Brett?'

'No. Everything is as it was when they removed my aunt's body.'

'We'll take it then, if you don't mind.' Millson handed the pad to Scobie. 'It should have been put with her suicide note as evidence. And where are your aunt's letters and papers, please?'

Tony Brett indicated two large bin-liner bags against the back door. 'You're only just in time, I was about to put them out for the dustmen. You'll find everything in there . . . letters, bills, old photos . . . the lot . . . There was no point in keeping anything.'

'We'll take them then,' Millson said.

'We'll call in at the local nick and pick up the case file,' Millson said as they loaded the bin bags into the boot of his car. 'Then we're going on to the lab.'

'What are you expecting to find out?' Scobie asked.

'That her note wasn't a suicide note and didn't mean what the coroner thought it did.'

'That would mean she was murdered!'

'Exactly,' Millson said grimly.

At the laboratory in Chelmsford a forensic scientist, Gavin Wasserman, peered at the pad of paper Millson handed to him and said cheerfully, 'Sort of cheap tear-off notepad you can buy at any stationer's, Chief Inspector.'

'I know that,' Millson said sourly, pulling Marjorie Wilson's folder from his case. He opened the folder and took out the suicide note. 'This was the last message written on the pad. I want to know if you can tell me what was written on it before that.'

'OK,' said Wasserman. 'I'll try an ESDA test.'

He carried the note and pad to a box-shaped piece of equipment on a table. He fixed the note to a sloping board with drawing pins and picked up the nozzle on the end of a length of tubing. Turning a switch he directed waves of fine black powder across the paper.

'The indentations are quite deep,' he said as more words began to appear on the paper. 'The writer was pretty agitated, I'd say.'

He stopped the machine, unclipped a ballpoint from the pocket of his white overall and began making notes on a clipboard. Then he removed Marjorie Wilson's note and repeated the process with the blank top sheet of the notepad.

At the finish, he brought the clipboard to Millson. 'It's quite a jumble,' he said. 'There are impressions from two previous messages. The only words I can make out from the first are: "where" and "money". The impressions left by the second one are clearer, although they've been partly overwritten. It's possible to deduce the sentence: "You're mistaking me for someone else."'

Wasserman waited while Scobie wrote it down. 'I'm not an expert on handwriting, but I would say the three notes were written by the same person,' he added, 'and probably soon after each other because all the writing shows the same signs of stress.'

'That's very helpful,' Millson said. 'Thank you.'

'If she wrote those three notes one after the other,' Millson said, fastening his seat belt, 'she was writing them *to* someone and that third one was no suicide note. Why write, though?'

'Perhaps she wasn't able to speak,' Scobie suggested. 'Perhaps she was gagged.'

Millson's hand dropped away from the ignition key. 'There are times, Norris, when you hit the nail bang on the head. Of course, *that's* what the note means. The *gag* is hurting her and she can't stand it.'

Millson started the car and went on: 'She was gagged to keep her quiet and then interrogated and made to write down her answers. In one she mentions money and in another she says she's being mistaken for someone else.

60

I think she was trying to talk herself out of trouble.'

'The man could have been a burglar who thought she had money stashed away.'

'No, I think he was accusing her of blackmail and she was pretending he'd got the wrong person,' Millson said. 'Either way, the man was a cold-blooded killer and clever enough to use her own words to fake a suicide.'

'Can the inquest be reopened?'

Millson sucked his teeth. 'No. There would have to be an application to the High Court for a new inquest. And that needs the approval of the Attorney-General. Not a chance with only this evidence.'

The following morning the incident-room staff began examining Marjorie Wilson's belongings. The bin bags were emptied onto tables and the mementoes, souvenirs, photographs . . . the accumulated paraphernalia of a lifetime . . . spread out for cold, professional scrutiny.

'It's possible this woman was blackmailing someone,' Millson told his officers. 'So, look for letters, newspaper clippings, diary entries and suspicious money transactions.'

Early on a WDC picked out Marjorie Wilson's phone bill for the last quarter and showed it to Millson. He was luckier than with John Dennison's. Phone calls in the Westcliff area were itemized.

'I want to know who the subscriber was on every one of those numbers,' Millson told the WDC.

Another WDC working through the bank statements spotted a deposit of five thousand pounds paid into the account a month ago. It stood out like a beacon among the entries of minor debits and credits.

'That could be a blackmail payment. Find out more about it,' Millson ordered.

The check on the numbers listed in Marjorie Wilson's phone bill revealed she had made three calls to John Dennison and four to the Labrams' number at Spencers. One of the latter had lasted forty-five minutes.

'Abigail Labram told us she'd lost touch with everyone and gave the impression she had only the one call from Marjorie Wilson,' Millson said. 'These four calls and her presence at the funeral give the lie to that. No wonder she was upset to see us there.'

Inquiries into the five-thousand-pound deposit established that it had been paid in at a London bank in cash for credit to Marjorie Wilson's account in Westcliff.

'Dennison worked in London,' Scobie reminded Millson. 'Perhaps he and Marjorie Wilson were in league and this was her cut.' He went on enthusiastically, 'She provided the dirt and he did the collecting.'

'It's an idea, but don't let it run away with you, Norris,' Millson said crushingly. 'Who was the woman Clark said knew everything about everyone?'

'Betty Foster. She lives in Blackheath.'

'Fix up a visit. Let's see if she can tell us what Marjorie Wilson knew that could be used for blackmail. If we can identify the dirt it should give us the victim and lead us to the killer.'

Betty Foster was puzzled by Scobie's phone call. She wondered why a police sergeant and chief inspector wanted to speak to her about the murder of John Dennison. She'd already had a visit from a detective constable a fortnight ago. These two had been at Midge's funeral. That puzzled her too.

Betty had been shocked and saddened by Midge's suicide. She'd known Midge since Bournemouth days. Nineteen-forty. She could remember it like yesterday.

How young they'd been. Sixteen, seventeen . . . barely out of school . . . working in Whitehall in the blitz. The railways and buses were in chaos and they couldn't travel back and forth to work, so they slept at the office and did first-aid duty and fire-watching.

The bombing got worse every night. There was a direct hit on the Treasury . . . then the War Office . . . Horseguards . . . and a bomb on the corner of Downing

Street. They kept going despite it all, even scampering across Whitehall at night to the Red Lion for a quick drink between raids. Then, suddenly, the decision to evacuate government departments.

Tuesday, November 12th. There was apprehension and fear tinged with excitement as they gathered at assembly points all over London, not knowing where they were going or what would happen next. There had been a special train waiting at Waterloo . . . she remembered the comfort of seeing familiar faces in the mêlée on the platform.

Then, arrival in Bournemouth and coaches dropping them off at addresses around the town. Being billeted like school children – the boys out at Boscombe, the girls and the senior staff in the town.

Waking up next morning to sunshine and peace. No air-raid sirens, no bombing, no sandbags round the buildings. Fresh sea air. Walking to work – she recalled the strangeness of that – in requisitioned hotels that had been turned into makeshift offices.

Christmas a few weeks later.

Betty Foster greeted Millson and Scobie with a polite smile. She was a lively, energetic woman with slightly protruding eyes and dark, wiry hair, turning grey.

'I hope this won't take long,' she said as they sat down in the front room of her semi-detached house in Blackheath. 'I have a keep-fit class at the community centre in three-quarters of an hour.'

Millson said good-humouredly, 'I don't imagine your health will suffer if you're late, Mrs Foster.'

She said tartly, 'Mine won't, but other people's will. I'm the instructor.'

Scobie hid a smile as Millson looked discomfited.

'No need to look so surprised, Chief Inspector,' she went on. 'I run classes for the elderly. Mind you, most of them are younger than me, but they prefer me to some sylphlike thirty-year-old teaching them. So, let's get on with it. One of your men has already asked me questions about John Dennison. Why this further visit?'

'I'm hoping you can help us with more information,' Millson said. 'I understand from Mr Clark you know most of the staff Mr Dennison brought together for the reunion.'

She nodded. 'I've been friends with some of them since the war. He wouldn't have been able to find them without me.'

'So, you know a good deal about them?'

Betty Foster gave him a keen look. 'Possibly. I hope you're not expecting me to gossip about them.'

'I'm only interested in what might have a bearing on the case,' Millson assured her. 'A file was stolen from Mr Dennison's flat on the night he was murdered. It contained sensitive personal information about the people he'd traced for the reunion and I'm concerned about the use to which that knowledge might be put.'

She frowned at him. 'What sort of sensitive information?'

Millson folded his hands across his stomach. 'About indiscretions, vices . . . crimes perhaps. Things people wouldn't want known about themselves.'

'I see,' she said slowly.

She was silent for a while. Betty Foster had reached a senior position in the department by the time she retired, one that brought her into frequent contact with high-ranking policemen. She was not to be hurried into cataloguing the misdeeds of her colleagues by a chief inspector.

At last she shook her head and said, 'I can think of nothing serious enough for blackmail – and I assume that's what you're thinking of. Not in the last ten or twenty years, anyway.'

'How about before then? I believe some of those who came to the reunion hadn't seen each other for fifty years.'

'Oh . . .' She looked surprised. 'You're asking about Bournemouth . . . that far back?'

64

Millson nodded. 'Shame can last a lifetime. People have been blackmailed over events in their childhood.'

'I see.' She looked thoughtful. 'In that case . . . there was something. Everyone was talking about it at the reunion.' She gave a faint smile. 'You'd think, after not meeting for fifty years, they'd find something more important to talk about than a party.'

'Tell me about it,' Millson invited.

'Very well.' She put her hands in her lap and leaned back in her chair. 'We were all very young – still in our teens – and there we were, away from home and suddenly free. Free of the bombing, free of our parents. The boys were being called up or had volunteered for the Forces, and everything was happening very fast. I think we crammed more into a week than normally happened in a month. We lived for the moment, you see, because we didn't know what would happen next. We all went a little wild.' She laughed self-consciously. 'I know I did.

'There was a Christmas party in one of the billets – a guesthouse called Larnaca, where a lot of the boys were billeted. A dozen or so of us girls went to it and some of the girls stayed the night. They slept in the beds of the boys who'd gone home for Christmas. I didn't. I went back to my billet with Charles – a boy I was going out with at the time.'

She paused. Then she said soberly, 'Something happened at Larnaca that night. There were rumours, but the girls wouldn't talk about it. They've never talked about it . . . not to me, not to anyone, so far as I know. Ask *them* about that party, Chief Inspector.'

'Them?' Millson queried.

She stared at him as though he were dense. 'You saw them at the funeral,' she said. 'Abby, Peggy, Rachel . . .' She gave a twisted smile. 'Even Midge, in a way. The four of them . . . they were all there.'

CHAPTER 8

When Millson returned from Blackheath there was a message on his desk asking him to phone John Dennison's mother.

'It's over a month since John was killed. How much longer do we have to wait to make arrangements for his funeral?' she asked when Millson rang her.

'I'm afraid the Coroner's Office aren't likely to release the body until someone is charged and criminal proceedings begin,' he explained.

'Why didn't you tell us that before? This is very distressing for me and my husband, Chief Inspector, and I'd have thought you'd have a little more concern for our feelings.'

Millson winced. He hadn't spoken to them since the father identified his son's body at the mortuary. There had been nothing he could say. It would only have added to their distress if he'd hinted he thought their son was a blackmailer and that was why he'd been murdered.

'I'm sorry I haven't been in touch, Mrs Dennison,' he said. 'Unfortunately we haven't made much progress and we still have a number of inquiries to make.'

'What sort of inquiries? We are his parents, you know. Surely you can tell us something?' she demanded.

'Well, we know your son went to the Oak Tree pub the evening before he was murdered. Witnesses say he seemed to be waiting for someone. We're trying to find out who.'

'Oh, I can tell you *that*,' Mrs Dennison said crossly. 'I expect he was waiting for Sarah – his girlfriend. At least,

I suppose she was his girlfriend, though he never brought her home to meet us.'

'He was meeting Sarah Howarth? What makes you say that?' Millson asked.

'Because he phoned us that evening.' There was a catch in her voice as she said, 'It was the last time I heard his voice. He was so pleased. He told us he was being promoted . . . it was in recognition of all the work he'd done on that reunion. He said he wanted us to be the first to know and then he was going to tell Sarah. From what he said, I'm sure he was meeting her later on. Anyway, why don't you ask her?'

'Oh, I will,' Millson said. 'I will. Thank you.'

He put down the phone and frowned. It was the first question he'd asked Sarah Howarth. She'd said she didn't have a date with Dennison. Why would she lie?

'Maybe his mother misunderstood,' Scobie said, when Millson recounted his conversation with Mrs Dennison. 'Or he changed his mind.'

'Possibly. All the same, we'll have another word with Sarah Howarth.' Millson made a face. 'That girl's attitude to her boyfriend's murder seems a little odd to me.'

Sarah Howarth's flat was as cheerless and unwelcoming as on their first visit. Scobie had now moved in with Kathy Benson and the contrast with Kathy's homely apartment in Tanniford was striking.

Sarah Howarth, wearing a long white shirt over blue denims, was as cool and detached as before. Millson approached the question he'd come to ask at a tangent. It was a habit of his when dealing with a witness he thought was devious.

'You said you didn't know much about Mr Dennison's work, but did he mention the reunion to you? The fiftieth anniversary he arranged in Bournemouth?'

She made a face. 'Oh, sure. He was always on about it and the terrific job he'd done. John thought it was wonderful, all those people meeting up after fifty years. I didn't. I mean . . . wallowing in nostalgia . . . drooling over things that happened yonks ago . . . it's creepy.' She hunched her shoulders in a shiver.

'Did he tell you he was going to be promoted for the work he'd done on the reunion?'

'No,' she said flatly.

'He heard the day before he was murdered. It would be the natural thing to do, wouldn't it? To meet you and tell you?'

She shrugged. 'I suppose so. What are you getting at?'

Millson fixed her with his eyes. 'His mother says he was in the Oak Tree that evening to meet you and tell you his good news.' He saw her eyelids quiver slightly, a mannerism of hers. There was no other reaction.

'Then she was wrong,' Sarah Howarth said firmly. 'I told you before, Chief Inspector, we didn't have a date that night.'

'Well, he was waiting for *someone*,' Millson said.

She said lightly, 'Then perhaps I wasn't his only love. He could have been meeting another girl, couldn't he?'

Millson said irritably, 'The first time we met you introduced yourself to me as John's girlfriend, Miss Howarth. Now you seem anxious to distance yourself from him. Or is it that you didn't really care for John Dennison?'

She bridled. 'That's unfair! I was simply making a rational suggestion.'

She didn't go on to say, 'Of course I cared for him,' or anything like that, though, Scobie noticed.

'Did John ever mention a Marjorie Wilson to you?' Millson asked.

She shook her head, the fair curls swaying. 'I don't think so. Was she another girlfriend?'

Scobie interjected with, 'Marjorie Wilson was sixty-eight, Miss Howarth.'

She shrugged. 'He could have been her toy boy.'

'Marjorie Wilson is dead,' Scobie said. 'She committed suicide.'

Her expression changed only slightly. 'Oh. Well, I'm sorry. No, he didn't mention her.'

Millson came to his feet. 'Well, thank you for your time, Miss Howarth.'

She seemed taken aback by the abrupt departure and at the door she said, 'I'm sorry I haven't been much help. I didn't mean to be rude.'

Millson turned. She'd sounded apologetic. 'That's all right,' he said gruffly.

She said meekly, 'May I ask you a question, Chief Inspector?'

'Of course.'

'D'you think John was killed by someone he knew, or by a stranger?'

'I don't have an opinion one way or the other at the moment, Miss Howarth,' he said. 'I can give you the statistics, though. Three-quarters of murder victims are known to their killer. Only a quarter are killed by complete strangers.'

'Thank you.' Millson wondered why she sounded relieved.

'And if you're interested in the other relevant statistics,' he added, with a faint smile, 'male homicide victims are usually knifed, shot, or beaten to death . . . not strangled. Only seven per cent die that way compared with twenty-five per cent of females.'

Following their interview with Betty Foster, Millson had made an appointment to see Abigail Labram and on the way the next morning he picked up Scobie from Kathy's flat.

This time she was alone when they were shown into the drawing room at Spencers. She was wearing a dark blue dress with white collar and cuffs and she looked annoyed as she rose to greet them.

'What is it now?' Her tone was imperious.

'Mrs Labram, the last time we were here I understood you to say you'd lost touch with your colleagues from

Bournemouth days and that's why you didn't go to the reunion.'

'That's right.' She forestalled his next question. 'You're wondering why I was at Midge's funeral?'

'Yes.'

'Midge and I were very close once. When Mr Clark phoned and told me of her death, the least I could do was to attend her funeral and pay my respects.'

'Quite so,' Millson said and went on smoothly, 'although her recent phone call to you was the first time you'd heard from her in years, I think you said.'

Her eyebrows came together slightly. 'Yes, that's right.'

'Yet my information is that Marjorie Wilson made several calls to your number in the last month.'

'How do you know that?' she asked quickly.

'Would you mind answering my question, Mrs Labram.'

'Mr Dennison was trying to arrange another reunion and Midge rang me to ask if I was interested. I said I wasn't.'

'They were long calls,' Scobie said. 'One of them lasted three-quarters of an hour.'

Her eyes turned towards him. After a brief pause she said, 'As I've said, we used to be close friends. We were catching up on each other's news.' She looked at Millson again. 'Surely you haven't come here just to ask me about telephone calls, Chief Inspector?'

'No, I haven't, Mrs Labram. I believe you were also friends with two others at the funeral. Peggy Pennington and Rachel Green.'

Her eyebrows arched in surprise. 'Yes. We shared a flat together in the war . . . Midge too.'

'I've been told there was another connection between the four of you.'

'And what was that?' she asked.

'You were all at a certain Christmas party,' he said and saw her eyes widen in alarm.

'Nineteen-forty, in Bournemouth,' he went on. 'At a place called Larnaca.' If he'd hoped to alarm her further

70

he was disappointed. She had herself under control again.

'Gracious me,' she said. 'So we were. What possible interest can that have for you?'

'So you were there?'

'You obviously know I was or you wouldn't be asking these questions. Though they're totally irrelevant.' Her tone was frosty and faintly hostile. The lady of the house putting down a servant for asking improper questions.

Millson pressed on. 'Did something happen at that party?' He realized how feeble it sounded as soon as he said it.

Her smile was slightly mocking. 'Oh, lots of things. We had Christmas dinner, party games . . . dancing . . .'

He said impatiently, 'Betty Foster implied something serious happened. That there's some secret the four of you shared.'

'What rubbish!' The smile became pitying. 'Betty always thought we kept secrets from her. She should have grown out of that by now. It's tiresome of her to set you off on a wild-goose chase.' Her tone became indignant. 'Really! I should have thought you had more serious inquiries than this to make.'

She was buoyant now. Some danger had been safely bypassed and Millson had no idea what it was.

'That explanation of hers about the phone calls from Marjorie Wilson was eyewash. I'm sure it wasn't true,' Millson said as they drove away from Spencers. 'What's more, she was frightened of what Betty Foster might have told us. Notice how she perked up when she realized we knew nothing? She's hiding some old scandal from us and it has to be serious else she wouldn't bother.'

'It might not be anything to do with the murders, though,' said Scobie, who felt Millson was attaching too much significance to Mrs Foster's remarks.

'That's what I want to find out. Look up the addresses of the other two.'

Scobie took out his copy of Kenneth Clark's list from

his briefcase and scanned it. 'Peggy Pennington and Rachel Green both live in Bournemouth,' he said.

'A day by the sea will make a nice change, Norris. And hopefully, they'll be more forthcoming than Abigail Labram.'

Sarah Howarth pulled on a dressing gown over her pyjamas and made herself a cup of drinking chocolate. Then she settled into an armchair in front of the television to watch the late evening news. She wanted to see if there was anything new on John Dennison's murder.

Yesterday's visit by the police had upset her, especially when that gorilla of a chief inspector criticized her feelings for John. He'd been right, of course, she didn't love John, but that wasn't his business. Her ability to give and receive love had been stifled a long time ago.

Sarah's father had been killed in a car crash when she was seven. Three years later her mother remarried and Sarah found herself with a stepfather. She disliked him from the beginning. He was sixty-one, a retired civil servant, and far too old for her mother who was twenty years younger. Her mother explained to her that he was a widower and she was a widow and by pooling their resources they would be better off. Sarah would rather have remained poor and be without this stranger in the house.

'Call me Artie,' he told Sarah, which was fine with her because no way was she going to call him 'Daddy'.

Young as she was, Sarah had the wisdom to hide her dislike of Artie. It was partly out of consideration for her mother, but mainly from a sense of self-preservation. She quickly learned that Artie had a violent temper and she was terrified of what he might do to her.

Although he didn't actually hit her, he didn't show her the slightest affection either. Not ever. His way of disciplining her was to fasten his hard blue eyes on her and speak in a cold voice that shrivelled her up inside. He was so menacing that sometimes she wet her pants in fright. And then he would smile his horrible smile and tell her to go and change.

He was obsessively tidy and tried to make Sarah the same. Periodically, he inspected her room, pulling open the drawers and wardrobe. If her clothes were not neatly folded and tidy he would say, 'Not good enough, Sarah. No pocket money this week.'

Her stepfather's idea of bedtime stories was to recount his experiences in the navy during the war . . . of men drowning in a sea of oil . . . of burning bodies and unspeakable injuries. When she was older she discovered he'd never been to sea and had served his time in the war as a clerk in the Admiralty pay office.

Artie had other quirks too. 'He's weird,' Sarah confided to a schoolfriend. 'He goes all peculiar when he hears a bluebottle in the house. He gets out the fly spray then shuts himself in the room with it and stands there giving it a little squirt every now and again. The bluebottle goes mad. It zooms around, hurling itself at the window, buzzing and whirring. It takes ages to die. You should see Artie's face as he watches it. Gives me the creeps.'

'Your stepfather's a sadist,' her friend said, 'that's what he is.'

A fact later confirmed by Sarah's discovery that Artie's collection of wildlife videos had nothing to do with an interest in animals. One day she caught him playing and replaying violent scenes of a pack of hyenas ripping the undersides from a wildebeest as it staggered about trying to escape.

Sarah left school at sixteen and took a job as a living-in housemaid at a hotel in Lowestoft. It was the first job she could find that would take her away from home. In her times off she attended classes in book-keeping and two years later she joined the accounts department of a firm in Ipswich and was able to rent a flat.

Sarah Howarth put down her drinking chocolate, stretched out a hand for the remote control and switched off the television. There had been no mention of the murder.

Her mother had died two years ago. She'd had a miserable life with Artie, Sarah reckoned, no warmth or love from him at all. The house – which Sarah's father had bought and paid for – her mother's personal possessions, savings account, all went to Artie.

'Your mum didn't make a will,' he told Sarah after the funeral. 'So everything's mine.'

He'd allowed her to take her mother's photo albums and books, but nothing else, not even an ornament. Mean bastard! Sarah sipped her drink.

A slow smile spread across her face. Ah well, she'd had the last laugh on that all right.

CHAPTER 9

Peggy Pennington and her husband lived in a detached house near Branksome Park. The house stood in a quiet residential road and had a large garden bordered with conifer trees.

As they stopped outside the house Millson nodded his head in the direction of the sea and said, 'That's Branksome Chine down there.'

Scobie gave him a blank look.

'Neville George Heath, 1946,' Millson said impatiently. 'Don't you know your criminal history? He met a girl in the Bath Hotel here, had dinner with her then took her for a romantic stroll down Branksome Chine. Five days later they found her body in the bushes. Heath had raped her and cut her throat.'

'That was his second murder,' Scobie said, to show he did know the case. 'They charged him with the first one and he was convicted and hanged.'

Millson nodded approvingly. 'They knew what to do with his sort in those days.'

Peggy Pennington was an ebullient woman with dark, curly hair. She was dressed in fawn slacks and a cream blouse. After briefly introducing her husband – a tubby, bald-headed man – she bundled him into the garden.

'Don't want him listening to everything,' she said cheerfully as she sat them down in the conservatory at the rear of the house. 'He'd only worry.'

Millson waited for an explanation of why Mr Pennington would worry, but she didn't give one and sat waiting for him to begin.

'Mrs Pennington, we think blackmail may be the motive behind John Dennison's murder. If we can discover the substance of the blackmail, that could lead us to his killer. Now, it's likely to be something that happened a long time ago, bearing in mind the probable age of the victim.'

'I don't see how I can help.'

'Mrs Foster mentioned a wartime Christmas party.'

'Good Lord!' Peggy Pennington snorted with amusement. 'Are people still on about that? We spent half our time at the reunion yacking about it.'

'It must have been some party,' Scobie said.

'Oh, it was. It was indeed.'

'Mrs Foster gave us the impression something unpleasant happened there,' Millson said.

'Trust Betty to stir things up. She's good at that.'

'Well, did it?' he asked.

'No, of course not. That's just Betty's imagination. She thought we kept things from her. Actually, I think she was jealous of the close friendship between the four of us.'

'The four being Midge, Abigail, Rachel and yourself?'

'Yes, we shared a flat at the Lansdowne. Didn't Betty tell you?'

'No, but I gathered that from Mrs Labram.'

'So, there you are, Chief Inspector. Betty's been wasting your time.'

'Tell me about the party,' Millson invited.

She laughed. 'You really want to know about the games we played fifty years ago?'

He nodded. 'I'm curious.'

'All right.' She stood up. 'If I'm going to reminisce about the past, I need a drink. Otherwise I'll start mooning over my lost youth. Will you join me?'

To Scobie's surprise Millson said, 'Why not? We've come a long way.'

Peggy smiled at him and the tension in her eased. She would waffle on about the games – well, some of them at any rate – and bore him stiff.

It had been marvellous meeting Abby again at the funeral. Pity about poor Midge, though. Depressed over losing her partner, they said. Midge had never had much luck with her men. Abby had taken Rachel and her to lunch after the funeral and they'd talked long into the afternoon. Abby had landed on her feet with Mike Labram. Oodles of money, apparently, and it couldn't have happened to a nicer girl.

Abby had phoned her this morning, worried about the police digging into the past and asking questions that had nothing to do with John Dennison's murder.

'Don't worry,' Peggy had told her. 'I'll head them off.'

She served the drinks and sat down again. Millson offered her his cigarettes and she took one. He lit it for her and she drew on it heavily, exhaling smoke through her nostrils.

'There was this game called "Winking",' she began.

It would be their last Christmas together. There was an air of foreboding and a desperate urge to enjoy themselves while they could. No one knew where they'd be next Christmas. Some of them would probably be dead. The boys had their call-up papers and many of the girls were joining up too. London was in ruins, their families in danger and who knew what fresh disasters the New Year would bring.

Peggy couldn't remember who'd organized the game. It had begun late in the evening when the party was hotting up. Chairs were brought from the dining room and set out in a circle facing inwards. The girls sat on the chairs – one chair being left vacant – and a boy stood behind each chair.

The game began with the boy behind the empty chair winking at a girl he liked. If she wanted to respond, she tried to leave her chair and run across to him and the boy behind tried to grab her shoulders and stop her. If he succeeded, she gave him a kiss and if she escaped the boy with the vacant chair got the kiss and she sat down on it.

The boy who'd lost her then had an empty chair and it was his turn to choose a girl. And so the game went on.

Except there were breaks for more drinks. Most of them were unused to drink, especially the girls, and there was no one to call 'Time!' and no waiting parent to worry about.

The party became rowdy . . . inhibitions loosened . . . and in a corner of the room a game of strip poker started.

Peggy didn't mention the strip poker. Since the girls were no good at poker, it had really been a compulsory striptease. And the version of the Winking Game she gave the two sober-faced policemen listening to her was an innocuous one.

'It was actually quite a subtle game,' she said. 'You see, it was up to the girl whether she answered a wink and to the boy behind her how hard he tried to prevent her. It all worked rather well and everyone had a good time.'

Scobie, who had been following her description with interest, asked, 'What about the girls who were left out – who never got winked at?'

She laughed. 'We girls were a bit smarter than that, Sergeant. If you were desperate you *pretended* you'd been winked at and made sure you got to the boy with the empty chair before anyone else did.'

Peggy stole a sideways glance at Millson. Good-oh, he was looking bored. Prattle enough to seem helpful and leave out the heavy stuff, that was the idea, and it seemed to be working. She ploughed on.

'Then there were forfeits – like a boy having to crawl round the floor and kiss all the girls' knees.' She giggled. 'That was just an excuse to see our knickers.'

Eventually, Millson stopped her. 'Mrs Pennington, nothing you're telling me amounts to something a person could be blackmailed over today.'

Oh, brother, but you don't know the half of it, she thought. It had nothing to do with John Dennison's murder, though, and she wasn't going to expose the other goings-on to him. Dear, dead past . . . let it rest in peace.

'No, I suppose not,' she said. 'Perhaps Rachel remembers more. I expect you're going to see her, aren't you?'

From the innocent tone of voice he realized Abby Labram had phoned and forewarned them both. 'Yes, we are,' he said sourly.

'Rachel isn't very well at the moment, Chief Inspector,' she said earnestly. 'Next March will be the fiftieth anniversary of the commando raid on St Nazaire. Her fiancé was killed there and Rachel never really got over it. She's going across for the ceremony and I think she's secretly dreading it . . . seeing the actual spot he was killed, you know.'

Peggy Pennington just hoped Rachel would hold up under a visit from the police and keep her mouth shut. Rachel and Pat had sloped off from the party and hadn't been there most of the time, so it shouldn't be too difficult for her.

Rachel Green lived on the third floor of a block of flats in Southbourne. After Peggy Pennington's light, airy house the flat seemed dark and claustrophobic. The walls were covered with pictures and photographs and every flat surface – the table, shelves, television, windowsill – was covered with ornaments and bric-à-brac. It was the opposite of the Spartan interior of Sarah Howarth's flat in Ipswich.

Rachel Green was Spanish-looking, with long black hair and dark, intense eyes. She wore a red satin dress with a silver belt and her face was unsmiling.

'I can't tell you anything,' she said when Millson asked her about the Christmas party. 'I spent the whole time with the boy I was engaged to. We were very much in love and we didn't take much notice of what went on in the dark around us.'

'In the dark?' Scobie queried. No one had mentioned darkness before.

She was suddenly confused. 'No, no I don't mean it was dark.'

She must be careful. It hadn't been dark at the party, that was later. Rachel Green had listened intently to Peggy's phone call while Millson and Scobie were driving from Branksome to Southbourne. To Peggy reminding her of her promise.

'That was fifty years ago,' Rachel protested.

'You promised never to tell. *Never*. Remember?'

Rachel remembered all right. *Swear*, that's what they'd said. And she'd sworn. Oh yes, she remembered. Perfectly. Like her memories of Pat.

Rachel became aware of the heavy-looking policeman with the close-cropped hair speaking to her, asking about the boy she'd been engaged to.

'He's dead,' she said flatly. 'He was killed in the raid on St Nazaire. The 28th March 1942.' She quoted the date parrot-fashion.

'I'm sorry,' Millson said.

She smiled sadly and her eyes went to a row of photographs on the wall. 'That's him,' she said, pointing to a young man in naval uniform. 'That's Pat.'

Scobie gazed at the faded photograph. 'He looks very young.'

'He was. We all were.' Her voice was edged with bitterness. 'He was nineteen when he died.'

There was an uncomfortable silence. Then Millson said awkwardly, 'Miss Green, I don't want to distress you about your fiancé, but I need to ask—'

'Pat was special,' she said suddenly. 'I didn't share him with anybody.'

Millson frowned. An odd comment, that. 'What about Abigail and Peggy? Did they pair up with a particular boy?'

How much was she supposed to let out? Peggy hadn't had time to tell her. Rachel became frightened. 'I don't remember,' she said. 'I told you, I don't remember anything.'

As Millson continued pressing her, she began to panic. She knew what it was she mustn't tell him. What could it matter now, though? *Swear, Rachel! Swear you'll never tell anyone . . . ever.* She'd given her word. For ever.

She was tired. She just wanted to be left in peace with her memories. Memories were all that mattered now. And if these men kept on at her, it would cloud her memories of Pat and she might not remember him properly any more.

'Leave me alone!' she cried. 'I'm not well. Go away!' Her pupils were unfocused, the dark eyes staring wildly.

'Mrs Pennington's right, that woman's not well,' Scobie said in the lift as they left Rachel Green's flat.

Millson grunted. 'Maybe. And maybe she was putting it on. One thing's for sure, they've ganged up on us. They've been phoning each other behind our backs.'

Millson was annoyed with himself. Three women old enough to be his mother and they'd thwarted him. He must be losing his grip.

'If they're this tight lipped fifty years on,' he continued, 'whatever they're not telling us must be damned serious.'

'Not necessarily,' Scobie said. 'What seems serious at their age could be quite trivial – like those silly kids' games.'

'They weren't kids' games the way they played them,' Millson said.

'Well, that's what they sounded like to me,' Scobie said loftily.

'Then you weren't listening properly.'

'What did I miss?'

Millson said patiently, 'It wasn't what Peggy Pennington said – it's what she didn't say. Just think about it. These youngsters were away from home . . . no one to restrain them . . . and having a last fling before they went off to war. Doesn't it strike you things may have got out of control?'

'No, I don't see it that way at all.'

Millson regarded him with a baleful eye. 'What's the matter with you, Norris? Sea air not agreeing with you?'

Scobie said uncomfortably, 'I think you're making too much of this and I don't believe it has anything to do with our murder investigation.'

Scobie seldom criticized Millson's judgement. He waited for the blast.

Millson only said mildly, 'It may seem like that to you, but I believe what they're hiding *does* have to do with the murders in some way.'

Later, driving through the New Forest, he said, 'I want you to do two things when we get back, Norris. Dig out the statement of that woman who said she saw Abigail Labram in the Oak Tree and ask her to call in and see me. And go through the statements of the pub witnesses and see if any of them mention a girl like Sarah Howarth.'

'You think she was there that evening?' Scobie asked in surprise.

'No, I want to make sure she wasn't.'

'If she was with Dennison, witnesses would have said so.'

'If they met, yes. Not if she was there at some other time.'

Penelope Troop was an aggressive woman of thirty or so with brown hair and large white teeth. She looked annoyed when Millson asked her why she thought it was Mrs Labram she'd seen in the Oak Tree.

'Because I've seen her in the yacht club with her husband, Mike Labram, haven't I? He's the guy who owns *Consuelo*.'

'A motor cruiser?' Scobie asked.

'No, a socking great yacht . . . takes up half the channel coming in round Island Point and everyone has to give way to her.'

'Have you actually been introduced to Mrs Labram?' Millson asked.

She glared at him suspiciously. 'No. Why?'

'I'm wondering if the lady you saw with Mr Labram in the club could have been a crew member and not his wife.'

She thought about it. 'That's possible, I suppose.' Then, 'Hang about, though,' she said. 'I saw the same woman on his arm going into the commodore's lifeboat supper last winter.' She sniffed. 'It's one of those "by personal invitation only" affairs.' She grinned wickedly. 'Still doesn't mean she was his wife, of course.'

Scobie scribbled in his notebook: *Yes it does* and pushed it in front of Millson. Scobie had attended similar functions at the club with Kathy Benson who was a long-standing member. The Labrams' invitation would have been addressed to 'Mr and Mrs' and a man of Labram's standing would not have taken a woman who wasn't his wife.

Millson read the note and nodded. 'The woman you saw in the pub, Mrs Troop . . . would you describe her, please?'

'Sixty plus, well-preserved . . . grey hair.'

'How was she dressed?'

'She was wearing a blue suit, I think.'

Scobie retrieved his notebook. 'Could you be more specific?'

She glanced at him in astonishment and Millson said quickly, 'We're anxious to account for everyone in the bar that evening.' He didn't want Penelope Troop telling people the police were interested in Abigail Labram.

'OK.' Mrs Troop screwed up her eyes in concentration. 'The suit was velvet . . . it was royal blue . . . and the jacket had black binding round the lapels and side pockets. The skirt was plain . . . pencil-shaped . . . and she had blue shoes and handbag.'

'An excellent description,' said Millson. 'Thank you, Mrs Troop.'

Millson had told Scobie not to make an appointment before they called at Spencers. At the door, he instructed the maid who answered to tell her mistress they wanted to speak to her alone.

Abigail Labram, in a grey and white woollen waistcoat and full-length black skirt, stood looking out of the long windows as they entered the drawing room.

She turned. 'This is very unexpected, Chief Inspector.' She didn't invite them to sit down.

Millson waited until the maid withdrew, then asked, 'Do you have a blue velvet suit in your wardrobe, Mrs Labram?'

Her eyebrows lifted. 'I beg your pardon?'

He repeated the question.

'Why do you ask?'

'Just answer me, please. Or I can question your staff if you prefer,' he said.

Her eyes lit up with anger. 'You'll do no such thing! Yes, I do have a suit like that.'

'Thank you,' said Millson. 'And does it have black binding around the lapels and pockets?'

'Yes, it does. Why?'

He said harshly, 'That's what Mrs Troop saw you wearing in the Oak Tree the night Dennison was murdered.'

'I've already told you, Chief Inspector, she's mistaken.'

'She has described *you*, she has described the outfit you were *wearing*,' Millson said relentlessly, 'and she saw the same woman accompanying your husband to the commodore's lifeboat supper. Or are you going to tell me that wasn't you either?'

Abigail Labram turned abruptly away from him to the window and stood looking out into the garden.

'Come, Mrs Labram, don't waste any more of my time,' Millson said sharply. 'Admit you were in the Oak Tree that evening. Or do you want me to call in more witnesses to identify you?'

She sat down suddenly on one of the window seats. 'No,' she said. 'No, please don't do that.'

'The truth then, please.'

She bent her head. 'This is rather embarrassing, Chief Inspector.'

He knew then exactly what she would say. And she did. She turned round in the chair, a guilty smile on her face, and said, 'I was meeting a gentleman friend, you see . . .'

Millson closed his mind against the warm eyes and soft voice. She'd lied to him and she was still lying. 'His name?' he demanded.

'What? Oh, I couldn't possibly—'

'His name and his address!' He'd had enough of being hoodwinked by charming older women. 'If not, I shall have to ask you to accompany me to the police station.'

'*What*?' Outraged, she jumped to her feet and faced him.

'I mean it,' Millson said grimly. 'I shall arrest you for obstructing police inquiries.'

She stared at him, wide-eyed with disbelief. Millson stared back, unwinking.

The confrontation lasted several seconds. Then she lowered her head and said softly, 'I'm being blackmailed.'

Scobie heard Millson's quiet sigh of satisfaction. Progress at last.

'Take your time, Mrs Labram,' Millson said gently, 'and tell me about it, please.'

'Yes.' She raised her head again. 'Shall we sit down?' She took her usual chair at the side of the marble fireplace.

Millson sat down next to her and not opposite as he'd

done before. Abigail Labram was a victim now, not a miscreant.

She rested her arms on the arms of the chair and looked up at a photograph of a family group on the mantelpiece. Scobie followed her eyes. A young Mike Labram had his arms round the shoulders of his wife and son.

Abigail Labram laid her head back against the chair. 'My son, Edgar, is not my husband's child, Chief Inspector. Neither of them know. They must never know. It would wreck *all* our lives.'

'We shall treat the information as given in the strictest confidence, Mrs Labram,' Millson assured her.

'Thank you.' She went on, 'Two months ago I had a phone call. The voice was high-pitched . . . it sounded as though he was speaking through some kind of device. He said he had information about Edgar which he thought Edgar – and my husband – should know. He said he wanted five thousand pounds to keep it to himself and that would be the end of the matter.'

'They all say that,' Scobie said.

She nodded. 'I expect they do. I realized what was coming and when he told me he knew Edgar wasn't Mike's son, I tried to bluff. I said it was untrue and neither of them would believe it. He just laughed.' She put her hands in her lap. 'He said he'd paid for genetic tests to be done on samples of their hair – God knows how he got them – which proved they weren't father and son.' She took a breath. 'That finished me. I agreed to pay. He said if I went to the police he'd send the evidence straight to my husband and son.'

'What instructions were you given for handing over the money?'

'I was to draw it in fifty-pound notes and he'd contact me again. He phoned a few days later and told me to put the money in an envelope and be at the Oak Tree pub in Great Horkesley at 9.15 the next evening. I was to drive there alone and park in the pub car park. The envelope was to be left in full view on the passenger seat and the car unlocked. I was to go into the bar, have a drink and leave again sharp at 9.30. From there I was to drive to the Albert pub on the Colchester bypass where I would receive further instructions. He said this was to satisfy himself I had the money and wasn't being followed. When I went out to the car at 9.30, the money was gone.'

'Did you notice anyone watching you while you were at the Oak Tree? In the car park or in the bar?'

'No, but then I wouldn't have. The bar was crowded and it was dark in the car park.'

'You didn't see John Dennison? He arrived there about the same time as you. I know you'd never met, but I expect you've seen his picture in the papers or on the telly.'

'Yes, and I don't recall seeing anyone like him there.'

'Who else knew your son wasn't your husband's child?'

'Only Midge Wilson. And she would never tell anyone.'

Millson ignored the 'Told you so' look on Scobie's face and asked, 'What about Edgar's real father? Surely he must know?'

'He doesn't.'

She was silent for a while. Then she rose from her chair and, looking away from them to the fireplace, began speaking in a monotone.

'He was an Australian airman – a sergeant air/gunner – curly dark hair and good-looking. He was based at Hurn and I met him at a New Year's Eve dance at the Bourne- mouth Pavilion. After the dance we went for a walk in the Winter Gardens...' She shrugged her shoulders. 'There was no time for relationships in those days. We made love.' She turned from the fireplace. 'He was killed a week later.'

She returned to her chair. 'Mike had just joined the RAF and was about to be sent overseas for flying training. We were more or less engaged and when I found I was pregnant I told him I wanted to be married before he went.' She gave a half-smile. 'He didn't need any persuad- ing. He came down on a 48-hour pass and we were married at Bournemouth registry office. We've been married for fifty years and we've been very happy.' She saw Scobie busily writing. 'Do you *have* to write all this down, Sergeant?'

Scobie stopped and looked sideways at Millson. Millson said, 'He does, Mrs Labram, and I'll have to trouble you to call in at the station later to sign a statement.'

She made a face. 'Oh, very well.'

'Why do you think the blackmail has started now when your son is what . . . fifty?'

'Fifty in September,' she said. 'I don't know. Perhaps it was that wretched reunion. The only thing they all had in common was their time in Bournemouth in the war. And that's what they talked about . . . endlessly. Midge told me.' Her tone was contemptuous. 'What they did . . . who with . . . who dated who . . . If there was gossip about me perhaps someone put two and two together, did some research, and decided to blackmail me.'

'So, who do you think it was?' Millson asked.

'I've no idea.'

'Doesn't it occur to you it could have been John Dennison?'

'No, of course not. It wasn't,' she said flatly.

'You sound very definite about that.' Millson was puzzled by her reaction.

'Well, just because he was at the Oak Tree at the same time as me doesn't mean . . .' She broke off in dismay. 'Do you mean that's *why* he was killed? He was a blackmailer?'

'We think so, yes.'

Her dismay turned to shock as the implication sunk in. 'You surely don't think I killed him?'

'No, I don't.'

To Millson's disappointment, the discovery of the blackmail victim had not led him to John Dennison's murderer. He would have suspected the husband or son except that if they knew of the blackmail they would know what it was about. And in that case, a threat to tell them would have no effect and the blackmail would fail.

'Dennison must have had another victim,' Millson said. 'Someone else like you who Marjorie Wilson told him about.'

'*What*?' Her voice rose angrily. 'Midge? She didn't. I *know* she didn't. You don't understand. I—' She broke off.

'Would you mind explaining?' Millson asked.

She couldn't, not without explaining the long phone call from Midge, and that was out of the question. Could Midge have betrayed her? Was that why she'd killed herself? Abigail hadn't found the reason given at the inquest very convincing. Memories of the past surfaced in her mind . . . dear, faithful Midge. No, Midge wouldn't have let her down.

Abigail said in a calmer voice, 'I meant you don't understand how close Midge and I once were, Chief Inspector. We were like sisters. She would never do a thing like that.'

'She seemed very sure about Marjorie Wilson,' Scobie said, over a beer in the Bell at Thorpe le Soken where they'd stopped for lunch.

'And about Dennison. I don't understand why. Also I find her story about the Aussie airman a bit hard to swallow. She's not like that.'

'You don't know *what* she was like at seventeen. She could have been a right little tart,' Scobie said.

'Possibly. But the way she told us seemed odd to me.'

'How d'you mean?'

'No feeling. No embarrassment . . . no guilt. Nothing. She could have been telling us about some other couple. Come to think of it, she probably was.'

'Why make up the story?'

'I don't know, and I couldn't very well cross-examine her about it.'

'If it's not true then another man is the father. And if he's married with a family, he could be blackmailed too. He might be the other victim.'

Millson nodded. 'And Peggy Pennington and Rachel

Green probably know who he is. They shared a flat with Abigail and Midge. Don't tell me girls living together wouldn't work out who the father is if one of them got pregnant.'

'They won't tell you, though,' Scobie warned.

'I know a way to unbutton their mouths,' Millson said ominously.

Millson chose Rachel Green because she was the weaker of the two women. He called on her without warning to catch her unawares and make sure she had no chance to consult with Abigail and Peggy.

It was two o'clock in the afternoon when she opened the door to them. She was wearing a dressing gown and her dark hair was unbrushed. When she saw who they were she tried to shut the door, but Millson had put his foot in it.

'This is important,' he said. 'We must speak to you, Miss Green.'

She let go the door and turned away with a helpless gesture of her shoulders. 'Come in then.'

She shuffled across the carpet in her mules and sank down on a sofa, waving them wearily to armchairs.

Scobie glanced around as he sat down. The curtains were half closed, making the flat seem even more claustrophobic.

Millson said, 'I want to ask you some more questions about your time in Bournemouth, Miss Green.'

'Not again!' she said agitatedly. 'It was a long time ago and I told you I don't remember.' It was the safest thing to say. Why hadn't Abby or Peggy warned her of this visit?

'Come now, you shared a flat with Abigail, Midge and Peggy, I believe? Near the Lansdowne, they tell me. You remember that, don't you?'

Millson's tone was compassionate. If Rachel Green's problems with her memory were genuine he would lead her gently and coax the information from her.

'Ye-es.'

'And Abigail had a baby while you were there? Her son, Edgar?'

'Oh no. I'd joined the Wrens by then. So had Peggy. We left not long after Abby was married. She stayed on in the flat with Midge after Mike went to Canada and we didn't even know she was pregnant until Midge wrote and told us she'd had a baby.'

Even her flatmates accepted the baby as her husband's, Millson realized. He was at a dead end. He consoled himself with the thought he'd probably been on a false trail, anyway. It was more likely Dennison and Marjorie Wilson's other victim was someone who'd attended the reunion in Bournemouth.

On his last visit Rachel Green had evaded his questions about Bournemouth. This time, Millson was determined to find out why.

'Tell me about that Christmas party, Miss Green.'

She stiffened, dark eyes staring at him from a white face. 'I told you, I don't remember much about it,' she said stubbornly.

'Listen to me, Miss Green,' he said firmly. 'A man has been murdered.'

'That's nothing to do with us, nothing to do with us,' she suddenly chanted, like a child in class.

'And your friend, Midge, is she nothing to do with you? She was murdered too, you know.'

Scobie's head jerked round in surprise. He'd wondered about Millson's threat to 'unbutton their mouths', but hadn't dreamed he'd come out with that. He glanced at Rachel Green. She was looking at Millson from the corner of her eyes – eyes filled with suspicion.

'No, she wasn't,' she said. 'Midge committed suicide.'

As Millson moved his head slowly from side to side she became worried. Midge murdered? No, that couldn't be right. This ugly-looking policeman was trying to trick her. Her mouth set obstinately.

'Then why hasn't it been in the news?' she asked.

'I'm telling you in strict confidence.'

You can say that again, Scobie thought. We'll be in dead trouble if she opens her mouth to the press.

Rachel drew her dressing gown around her more tightly. She wished she could phone Peggy and ask her advice. 'Does Mrs Pennington know Midge was murdered?'

'Not yet.'

Why had he told her first? He was cunning, this police-man. And his eyes were on her all the time. She could feel them boring into her brain, trying to read her thoughts.

Millson became impatient. This woman was holding back something, he could tell from the way her eyes were darting round the room avoiding his. He leaned towards her and said brutally: 'She was strung up by the neck with her own clothesline, Miss Green.'

Rachel's eyes glazed with shock. 'Why are you telling me this?' she whispered.

'To make you understand the seriousness of withhold-ing information from me. I believe your friend Midge was murdered because of what she knew. Now . . . come along. The Christmas party. After the Winking Game . . . what came next?'

Her dark eyes stared at him. In the same low whisper she said, 'We played "Goodnight Sweetheart". It was the last game.'

The girls who were staying the night at Larnaca had slept in the beds of the boys who'd gone home for Christ-mas. Abby, Rachel, Midge and Peggy were in a bedroom on the second floor. The lights were out, the blackout shutters were up at the windows, and the building was in total darkness.

In the game, a boy fumbled his way to a bed, knelt down and gave the girl in it a goodnight kiss. If she guessed who he was she said, 'You're so-and-so. Goodnight, sweet-heart,' and he moved on to another girl. If she guessed wrong, or didn't say, he moved on top of the bedclothes and kissed her again. If she still didn't say anything or guess correctly, he got into bed with her.

'It was just kissing and cuddling,' Rachel said in a singsong voice. 'The girl nearly always knew who it was and only pretended she didn't if she wanted the boy to go further.'

Rachel's eyes fluttered and closed. She felt the tingle of a long dead excitement. Her mind drifted away into memories and sensations she hadn't experienced in years. Warmth . . . Pat's arms enfolding her . . . his lips on hers. Peace . . . happiness . . .

Vaguely she heard a voice saying, 'Go on, Miss Green.' Rachel went on . . . her mouth moving . . . no sounds coming out.

Scobie regarded her with consternation. She seemed to be in a trance. Had Millson sent her over the edge?

The past had become the present to Rachel Green. Four boys in the room. Solid blackness. Midge giggling in the bed under the window . . . Peggy snorting rude remarks in the corner bed . . . and quiet, insistent movements in Abby's bed against the wall . . .

Suddenly, the memory she'd kept imprisoned leapt out at her . . . overwhelming her with guilt and horror . . . bursting out through her mouth. Her eyes flew wide and she screamed, making Scobie and Millson jump.

'Abby was raped! *Raped*! In the bed next to me! And I didn't know it was happening. I . . . didn't . . . know,' she sobbed.

CHAPTER 11

Albert Smedley whistled cheerfully as he drove through Wakes Colne on his way to Brightlingsea. Rene had become more agreeable since Dennison's murder – even came out for a drink with him one evening. The murder had shaken her. Made her realize how chancy life was, she told him. You had to grab what was going while you could. Bert had high hopes he and Rene would soon be setting up home together again.

On the other side of Colchester he took the Clacton road and turned off it at Tenpenny Heath. In the back of his Toyota van was an oak draw-leaf table he was delivering to a customer in Brightlingsea. The table had been made to special order, with barley-twist legs, which had given Bert Smedley an excuse to mark up the price considerably. Four hundred pounds, he was charging. Cash.

'That's without VAT, see,' he told the customer. 'If you wants to pay by cheque I'll have to add on the VAT.'

They always fell for it, Bert found. He'd already added VAT to the price and as he didn't include cash sales in his VAT returns, he ended up with a handsome profit.

After he'd made the delivery he'd have a quick drink in Brightlingsea to celebrate, then call in on Rene on his way home. A smirk spread over his face. Rene should be even more accommodating today when he fluttered four hundred quid in front of her eyes.

In Brightlingsea, he brought the van to a halt outside a house in the High Street. Stepping down from the cab, he noticed a Volvo Estate parked on the forecourt of solicitors' premises on the other side of the street. As he manoeuvred the base of the draw-leaf table from the rear of the van, he glanced again at the vehicle. It was silver in colour, with an overlong roof rack. A familiarity in the outline tugged at his memory.

Inside the solicitors' offices one of the partners, Edgar Labram, looked up as his secretary knocked and entered. His eyes followed the movements of her slim figure as she placed a file in his in-tray and went out again. She was a pleasant contrast to his ex-wife, Val, who had been his secretary until she began divorce proceedings two years ago.

The decree nisi had been granted at the end of last year and Edgar was on the lookout for a new companion. Not as a wife or a living-in partner, though. That would expose him to the risk she'd latch on to half his assets one day, as Val had tried to do. He'd thwarted her in the end, but it had been a near thing. He wouldn't make that mistake again, not with the considerable inheritance coming his way when Mike Labram died.

Edgar Labram winced at the memory of the nasty shock he'd been given over his expectations a couple of months ago. His mother had called him into the library one evening after dinner and told him Michael Labram was not his father.

'I hoped I'd never have to tell you,' Abigail said.

'Who is my father then?' Edgar asked, when he recovered from the shock.

She averted her face. 'He's dead. He was killed in the war . . . soon after we met.'

Abigail enhanced and softened the stark explanation she'd given Millson. She painted a picture for Edgar of a brief and wildly romantic liaison with an Australian airman who had been killed in a raid over Germany. She came to the end of her story and studied his expression.

'You don't seem very upset.'

Edgar wasn't upset at all. He found he didn't mind not

being Michael Labram's son. He had little in common with him and they had never been close. His real father had been a sergeant air/gunner . . . shooting down Germans . . . killed in action. Edgar much preferred him to stuffy old Mike Labram.

'It's a shock, Mother, but it's not that bad.'

'Oh, good.' Abigail gave a sigh of relief. 'I'm so glad.'

'You must have married Mike pretty soon after my father was killed.' His tone was disapproving.

She lowered her head. 'I had to. Edgar, my dear, you can't understand what it was like then for an unmarried girl to have a baby. Mike loved me and wanted to marry me so there was no harm done. And it was the right thing for you.'

'Couldn't you have told him?'

She shook her head. 'Much as he loved me, he wouldn't have married me.'

'I don't understand why you're telling me this now.'

'Because someone has found out and wants to hurt us. I didn't want you to hear it from a stranger.'

'Who?'

'I don't know. It was just a voice on the phone.'

'You're going to tell Mike about me now, of course?'

'No. And he must never find out. I want you to understand something, Edgar. Mike has very rigid ideas about family and blood ties. He wasn't like it when he was young, but as he grew old and rich he became interested in his family history. He made a family tree and started tracing his ancestors.' Abigail sighed. 'I suppose it comes from having so much wealth. Heredity and "the blood line", as he calls it, are an obsession with him. No one who isn't a blood relative counts as far as he's concerned and if he discovered you were not his son . . . his blood . . . he would cut you out of his will. Believe me, I know what I'm talking about.'

There was another, even stronger, reason for Mike to disinherit him, but she didn't have to explain that to him, thank heaven.

She added, wryly, 'He'd probably cut me out too for deceiving him all these years. He'd leave everything to his brother.'

That had been Edgar's second shock. The third came a few days later. He suspected his mother had not told him everything about this voice on the phone. Whoever it was had probably made threats . . . asked for money.

Covertly, he kept watch on Abigail in the days that followed and when she unexpectedly visited her bank in Colchester he stayed home from his office, pretending a stomach upset. Supposedly in bed in his wing of the house, he listened in on his extension to every phone call.

He overheard his mother telling the artificial voice she wouldn't pay and she'd told her son the truth about his father. The voice threatened to tell Mike, and his mother gave in. Edgar listened carefully to the instructions for handing over the money and that evening he trailed his mother's Peugeot to the Oak Tree at Great Horkesley.

He lagged well behind to allow her time to park and enter the pub before him. As he was backing the Volvo into a parking space a red Lotus Esprit shot into the car park and parked in the vacant space beside his mother's Peugeot. Edgar caught a glimpse in his rear-view mirror of the young man stepping out from the Lotus.

Edgar finished parking and walked back past his mother's car. He glanced in at the passenger seat. The envelope of money was gone.

He looked around. The man from the Lotus was hurrying towards the pub. Edgar ran after him. As the man reached the entrance and pushed open the door, the light illuminated his face. Edgar recognized him and stopped.

He'd seen the man at Spencers last summer. His name was John Dennison and he was the secretary of some retired staff association. Dennison had spent the afternoon with Mike, asking questions and writing notes. He said he was gathering information for a reunion and was trying to trace and interview all the staff who'd been evacuated to Bournemouth in the war. Edgar realized that was how he'd learned about his mother. Someone had gossiped.

Edgar returned to his car and waited. He saw his mother drive away at 9.30 and Dennison emerge and drive away not long after. Edgar followed the Lotus in his Volvo, hanging on to the rear lights as it sped towards Colchester. He was only saved from losing it by the speed restriction beyond Horkesley Heath, where Dennison slowed down.

Cruising down the hill towards Colchester station, the Lotus's brake lights suddenly blazed and it turned into the driveway between two houses. Edgar stopped and eased the Volvo into a space between two parked cars on the opposite side of the road. As he switched off the engine, Dennison emerged from the driveway and entered the front door of the house flanking it.

Edgar left his car and crossed the road. The house was a cheap post-war semi with box-shaped bay windows. The wooden front gate was open and hanging off its hinges. He sauntered up the short path to the door and read the card pinned beneath one of the bell pushes: FLAT 2 (UPSTAIRS) JOHN DENNISON.

Stepping over the low wall into the drive, Edgar walked quietly to the rear of the house and through an open gate into the garden. At the rear of the house there were lights on upstairs. He trod softly down the lawn to the bottom of the garden and looked up at the windows. One room was a kitchen. In the other – a living room – Dennison was on the phone.

Edgar retraced his steps across the garden and along the driveway. He paused at a sash window he'd noticed at the side of the house and scrutinized the catch. Then he returned to his car and settled down to wait.

He was certain Dennison wouldn't be satisfied with five thousand. He'd be back again and again, a constant threat to his inheritance. Edgar had already made up his mind to kill him. It was now a question of how and when.

At half past midnight, the upstairs front room, which he judged to be Dennison's bedroom, was still in darkness and the downstairs lights of the house were on. A man, walking unsteadily along the pavement, turned in through the gate and went up to the bay window. Edgar Labram watched him make an attempt to peer through the closed curtains and then turn and disappear into the darkness at the side of the house.

A husband returning home late? Or did Dennison have a flatmate? Edgar bit his lip with frustration and continued waiting. Half an hour later the man reappeared and lumbered off down the road. Soon after, Edgar heard a vehicle being driven away.

Patiently, he maintained his vigil. He'd now decided how he would kill Dennison and passed the time rehearsing the details in his mind.

Suddenly, the lights came on in Dennison's bedroom. Edgar checked his watch. One o'clock. He'd allow an hour.

At two o'clock, he clambered into the rear of the Estate and emptied out the plastic bag in which he kept polish and rags for the car. He stuffed the bag and a screwdriver into his pocket and pulled on his driving gloves. Making sure no one was about, he stepped out of the car, crossed the road and melted into the shadows at the side of the house.

It gave Edgar relief and pleasure to take hold of Dennison's throat and feel it pulsating against his thumbs as he dug them into the windpipe. His plan worked perfectly and Dennison died easily, hardly making a sound.

Afterwards, he looked for the money, expecting to find it without difficulty. When he couldn't locate it, he began a thorough search. He was hampered by having to work quietly though, to avoid waking the woman downstairs, and in the end he gave up.

During the search he came across a file containing letters and notes about the people Dennison had traced for the reunion. Edgar brought the file away with him in case there was a reference in it to his mother or himself.

After he'd delivered the table and collected his money, Bert Smedley crossed the High Street and took a closer look at the Volvo. He half closed his eyes, envisaging its silhouette in the gloom of streetlights. It seemed exactly like the one he'd seen across the road from Rene's on the night of the murder. His eyes flicked down and noted the number.

He glanced at the solicitors' premises, a converted shop with screened windows. The Estate probably belonged to a client. Maybe he was asking advice about divorce. The man sitting hunched in the driving seat had been watching the houses. Or perhaps the car belonged to a private eye who worked for the solicitors.

Bert Smedley shrugged. If the police hassled him again he'd give them the number, but otherwise it wasn't his business and he certainly wasn't one to help the police. He recrossed the road and climbed into his van.

Edgar Labram watched him through the smoked-glass window of his office. He'd been keeping an eye on him from the moment he noticed him staring at his car. He wasn't certain, but he thought this could be the man he'd seen hanging around Dennison's house that night. Had he recognized the car? He couldn't have seen the registration number before because the car had been nose to tail between two other vehicles on the other side of the road. Perhaps it wasn't the same man and his interest in the car was just coincidence.

There was a hand-painted sign on the side of the van: ALBERT SMEDLEY, MAKER OF FINE FURNITURE. Edgar reached for a notepad and jotted down the address. Just in case.

CHAPTER 12

Norris Scobie had been shocked by Millson's treatment of
Rachel Green. 'You put that poor woman through the
wringer, George,' he said accusingly as they left her flat.

He used Millson's first name to signal his depth of
feeling. Millson objected to the usual form of address,
'guv'nor'. Schools and prisons had governors, he told
Scobie. He was a chief inspector. And 'sir' was only for
when senior officers were around. 'George' would do, he
said, but Scobie tended to limit it to particular occasions,
like now.

'I had to make her talk,' Millson said.

'And where did that get you?'

'It got me a possible blackmail victim and therefore a
suspect, that's where it got me,' Millson said sharply.
'What's more, it explains why Abigail Labram was so
unwilling to answer questions about the party.'

On his return from Bournemouth George Millson ate a
hurried meal and set off for a parents' evening at Dena's
school. He was not looking forward to it. He resented
teachers half his age lecturing him on his daughter's progress, or lack of it, in the various subjects. And he objected
to being spoken to as though he were halfwitted and
needed everything explained twice in words of one
syllable. Worse, as smoking was forbidden, he'd have to
endure the whole three hours without a cigarette.

It didn't make him any more cheerful to see Dena in
deep conversation with Julie when he arrived. Julie
looked like a fugitive from St Trinian's in her short school

skirt and bulging blouse. Dena hadn't mentioned her lately and he'd assumed they were no longer friends.

He managed to survive the evening, queuing for one teacher after another like a customer in a post office, without losing his temper. After he'd covered all her subjects, he whisked a protesting Dena out to the car.

'We were supposed to stay for a talk by the headmistress,' she said, rummaging in the glove compartment and bringing out a half-eaten bar of chocolate.

'I've had enough preaching for one evening.' He lit a cigarette and started the engine. 'Was that Julie's mother with her?' He'd noticed a young woman shepherding Julie around.

'No, that's her older sister. Julie's like me, she hasn't got a mother.'

'You have got a mother. You just don't live with her.'

'Julie's one is dead.' Dena popped a lump of chocolate into her mouth.

'I'm sorry. Why didn't her father come, then?'

'He's busy.'

Burgling or in prison, Millson thought.

She broke off another piece of chocolate and pushed it between his lips. 'You worry too much, Dad. What did old Maidenhead say about my maths?'

'Who's Maidenhead?' he mumbled through the chocolate.

'Virginia Head, our maths teacher. Virgin head, see?'

'She said your work was good, but you could do better.'

'That's all right then.' She wriggled down in her seat. 'I'm hungry. Can we go to McDonald's?'

Millson turned into the long gravel drive leading to Spencers next morning with a feeling of misgiving. Rachel Green had become hysterical when he tried to question her further.

'Ask Abby! Ask Abby!' was all she would say.

Questioning Abigail about the rape was likely to be distressing for her. Millson had considered bringing a woman police officer with him but, in the unusual circumstances, had decided to speak to Abigail Labram on his own.

He needed to find out which boy it had been, and where he was now. He would be nearly seventy today, which made it unlikely he could have strangled Dennison himself. However, contract killings were not unusual in domestic murder cases these days – there had been three in the past year alone. The going rate seemed to be around ten thousand pounds.

Abigail Labram's expression was tense when he was shown into the drawing room. She stood in front of the marble fireplace, fiddling with her pearl necklace and waiting for him to speak.

Millson struggled with conflicting emotions. He needed the information that only she could give, and he also wanted to spare her pain.

He said sombrely, 'I'm afraid I have to ask you about a rather delicate matter, Mrs Labram.'

Her grey-blue eyes flinched. 'That has nothing to do with your investigation! Nothing! It's private and I don't want to talk about it.'

As he'd expected, Rachel Green had already phoned and forewarned her. 'Please bear with me, Mrs Labram,' he said gently. 'I wouldn't intrude on your privacy if I didn't think it necessary. But I'm investigating murder and blackmail and from information I have received—'

She interrupted him. 'Bullied out of poor Rachel, you mean! She's told me how you frightened her to death by telling her Midge was murdered. How could you, Chief Inspector? I have a good mind to lodge a formal complaint against you.'

'If you'd been open with me in the first place I wouldn't have needed to question her at all,' he said quietly. 'I understand why you weren't, but it has made my job more difficult. As regards Marjorie Wilson, I have reason to believe she *was* murdered, though I can't prove it.'

She frowned. 'Why on earth would anyone murder harmless little Midge?'

'Because, as I said before, she was involved in blackmail with John Dennison.'

'You're wrong about Midge! And I think you're wrong about Mr Dennison too.'

Millson said firmly, 'Could we return to the purpose of my visit, Mrs Labram? And I'd like the truth this time, please.'

'Rachel has already told you what happened. You want to make me say it?' She turned and put her hands on the mantelpiece, leaning against it. 'All right! I was raped at that party.' She whirled round, her eyes angry and tearful. 'Are you satisfied? I hope you're pleased with what you've done . . . raking up nightmares from the past and causing misery to me and my friends . . . just to satisfy your police-man's prying mind.' She was struggling to hold back the tears. 'Now, if that's all . . .'

'I'm afraid it isn't,' he said.

'What more do you want from me?'

'I want his name.'

Her eyes grew enormous, gazing at him in horror. 'For pity's sake, why?'

'He too was probably being blackmailed . . . over what he did to you. That gives him a motive for murder and makes him a suspect. So, I need his name, please.'

She looked down at the floor and said in a tight voice, 'I didn't know then and I don't know now.'

Taken aback, Millson said angrily, 'I find that impossible to believe!'

She looked up. 'Do you now? Do you really? Didn't Rachel explain the game to you?'

'Yes, but there must have been a row about it afterwards . . . an investigation?'

'No!' She shook her head agitatedly. 'You don't under-stand! It was a different world then. I was very young . . . I couldn't face the shame and embarrassment of everyone knowing. I just wanted it kept quiet. And it was. No one knew, except Midge, Peggy and Rachel. Until you started

104

poking and prying with your questions.' She drew in her breath. 'Now, please go.'

After Millson left, Abigail Labram went upstairs to her bedroom. She rarely smoked these days, but now she took a cigarette from the silver box on her dressing table, lit it and inhaled deeply. Memories flooded in on her, unbidden.

Abby Coran, she'd been then. Seventeen. She remembered how glad her parents had been when she was evacuated to the safety of Bournemouth. Glad too when she told them she was sharing a flat with three of her friends. The tiny flat – four beds in one room – reminded Abby of the room she'd shared at her convent school. It had been fun deciding things for themselves, cooking their own meals and doing as they pleased.

Despite the war it had been a strangely happy time, those first weeks away from the gloom and turmoil of London. Walking along the seafront . . . going to the cinema – the cinemas in London had all been closed . . . dances at the Pavilion. Abby loved dancing.

Then, Christmas. Abby drew heavily on her cigarette, gazing at her reflection in the dressing-table mirror. The four of them invited to the party at Larnaca. Getting ready . . . giggling about spending the night there . . . wondering which boys had gone home for Christmas and whose bed they'd be given.

The weather had been cold and frosty, with a light fall of snow. They had walked along the seafront to Boscombe, exhilarated by the raw air, and arrived at the party pink-cheeked and bright-eyed. Someone had managed to procure a sprig of mistletoe and pin it over the front door. That was when Mike Labram first kissed her, Abby remembered. Tall, fair-haired and good-looking, he was one of the boys lining the entrance and demanding kisses as they arrived.

After the Christmas dinner there was music and dancing in the large common room and then games: postman's knock, blind man's buff, competitions . . . and forfeits. Abby felt a thrill of excitement in one of the forfeits, when Mike Labram smiled up at her as he caressed her knees with his lips.

Later, when he winked at her in the Winking Game, she wrested herself free of Bill Smith who was standing behind her chair and ran across the circle to him. She returned his kiss enthusiastically, her tongue probing his mouth, and realized with amusement it was a new experience for him. For the rest of the game, she made only token attempts to escape from Mike's grasp on her shoulders when boys winked at her. Every time he prevented her, she had to kiss him and their kisses became longer and more passionate as the game progressed.

By the time the girls went up to bed and the 'Goodnight Sweetheart' game began, Abby was heady with drink and anticipation. Midge, Rachel, Peggy and herself were together in one bedroom. They undressed, the lights were switched off, and in the darkness of the blacked-out room there were whisperings and mutterings as the first boys entered. Then, amid suppressed giggles, the creak of bedsprings in the government-issue beds.

Abby easily identified the first two boys who knelt by her bed to kiss her goodnight and passed them on, eagerly awaiting Mike Labram whom she intended to keep for a long time. She felt disappointed when he was not one of the next two boys either and wondered, jealously, if he was in bed with Joyce Bond who'd been making eyes at him all evening.

There was a sound near her bed, the bedclothes were lifted and she felt a body getting in beside her. A voice whispered, 'What's your name?'

This was against the rules of the game but, thinking it was Mike, she whispered, 'Abby.'

A hand clamped her mouth, the other enclosed her throat, and legs closed either side of hers like pincers. 'Keep quiet or I'll choke you,' he hissed, pulling the blankets up over their heads.

106

Terrified, she lay still. The hand left her mouth . . . delved down and yanked up her nightie. She arched, and the hand on her throat tightened warningly.

In the other beds there were gurgles of laughter and sounds of noisy kissing. In Abby's, only the rustle of bed-clothes as he silently raped her.

It was quickly over and in the blackness he slipped away as quietly as he'd come. Abby lay shocked and trembling, muffling her sobs with the blankets.

Abigail Labram finished the cigarette and lit another. She recalled the pain and degradation . . . reaching across to Midge's bed and seeking her hand. Drawing her out of bed and into her own . . . whispering what had happened.

Midge had taken charge. She'd turned on the lights, shooed Peggy and Rachel's partners from the room and told everyone the game was over and they were going to sleep now. Then she'd locked the door and the four of them had huddled together on Midge's bed.

'Who was it?' Midge demanded.

'I don't know,' Abby said tearfully. But she did.

Peggy said in a practical tone of voice, 'Well, if we find out who was with who and where, and put our heads together, we should be able to work it out.'

'No! I couldn't bear it,' Abby said. 'Not everyone knowing.'

They had argued with her for a long while, but Abby was adamant and in the end they had accepted her decision.

'I want a solemn promise from each of you,' Abby said, her voice strengthening as she made up her mind not to let this awful thing ruin her life. She switched off the lights and took down the blackout shutters from the windows.

Then, in the early light of dawn, three young girls swore in turn never to breathe a word to anyone about what had happened to Abby Coran that Christmas night.

*   *   *

107

Edgar Labram had been alarmed when the police came to Spencers a fortnight after the murder and questioned his mother on her whereabouts that night. They said a woman in the pub had recognized her. Edgar hung on every word of the interview, fearing his mother would confess to the blackmail. It had been all he could do to hide his relief when they accepted her explanation and alibi. He'd thought he was safe.

A fortnight later, though, there had been a phone call to his office. Edgar went cold as he heard the same distorted voice as he'd listened to giving instructions to his mother.

'Five thousand pounds, unless you want to lose your inheritance of several million.'

'My mother has already paid five thousand,' Edgar snarled down the phone.

'That's right,' the voice said. 'Now it's your turn.'

'I need time to get the money!' And time to find out who this was. Dennison must have had an accomplice.

'No you don't,' the voice said coldly. 'Have the money in a sealed package at your office at midday tomorrow. Address it to yourself at Spencers. A courier will call to collect it. He won't know anything, so don't bother questioning him. And don't have him followed or the package will be delivered to your house and we'll have to do this all over again.'

Edgar Labram bit his lip in vexation. Presumably the courier would be contacted by mobile phone and rerouted before he reached Spencers.

'All right,' he said through his teeth. He had no choice but to pay.

Edgar believed his mother would have an idea who Dennison's accomplice might be, but he couldn't ask her outright without revealing he was aware of the blackmail. So he asked her who knew he was not Michael Labram's son.

'No one,' she assured him. 'Well, only Midge and she would never tell anyone.'

'Midge?'

'Marjorie Wilson. She was a very dear friend of mine. We shared a flat during the war and she looked after me when I was having you.'

'Have I met her?'

'No. She hasn't seen you since you were a baby.'

'Are you sure no one else knows?'

Abigail frowned. Why was he asking these questions? 'Absolutely. Why?'

'When you told me about my father, you said there had been a voice on the phone.'

'Oh . . . that.' Abigail floundered.

'Yes. Do you know who it was?'

'No.' She did know, but she couldn't tell him. Any more than she could tell him about the blackmail. She realized from his expression what he was thinking. 'Whoever it was didn't find out about you from Midge,' she said quickly. 'She would never tell anyone.'

The threat had ended now, but she couldn't tell him that either. She tried to reassure him. 'Edgar, please don't worry. I've heard nothing more and I'm sure I won't.'

'Good.' Edgar forced a smile and nodded.

He was certain that Dennison and this woman, Marjorie Wilson, had been in the blackmail together. She had provided the information and he'd done the rest. And now she was carrying on the blackmail herself. He'd soon put a stop to that. She must be the same age as his mother and it shouldn't be difficult to shake a confession out of her.

He looked through the file he'd taken from John Dennison's flat and found her address. She was a 'Miss' and lived in Westcliff. A few days later he set up a meeting with a client in Southend to cover himself, and called at the house on his way. Marjorie Wilson was out.

Several of Edgar Labram's clients had been burglars and he used the knowledge he'd picked up, forcing the lock on Marjorie Wilson's front door with a credit card. While he was searching the house for evidence of her guilt, she returned. He tied and gagged her and continued the search. He found the proof he was seeking in her last bank statement – a deposit of five thousand pounds a day or two after he'd killed Dennison. That was why he hadn't found the money in his flat. Dennison had passed it to Marjorie Wilson in the pub.

The silly woman had tried to bluff – said she didn't know where the money came from. A good one, that! So he'd rigged a length of cord over the banisters to stretch her neck and make her confess. She'd been chattering away, making excuses, when she suddenly said she knew who he was and he'd had to finish her. He didn't understand how she recognized him, though, if she hadn't seen him since he was a baby.

Fortunately, it had been easy to make it look like suicide. Now he was safe again and could make plans for his future. With luck, Mike wouldn't live too long.

CHAPTER 13

In the incident room at Colchester police station a DC answering the phone asked the caller for his name.

'Never mind that. D'you lot still want to know 'bout the car what was across the street the night Dennison was done in?'

The DC put his hand over the mouthpiece and called across the room to a colleague. 'There's a guy asking if we're still interested in that car parked opposite the house. He won't give his name.'

'Tell him yes and tape what he says.'

The DC switched on the tape recorder attached to his phone and tried again to obtain the man's name. 'Your name, please?'

'I told you . . . I ain't giving it. D'you wanna know or not?'

'Yes, we do.' The DC heard a click and then the dialling tone. 'He's hung up,' he told the other DC in disgust.

Bert Smedley emerged from the phone box in Halstead looking thoughtful. A day or two after spotting the Volvo it had occurred to him he might turn the knowledge to his advantage, although only if the owner hadn't answered the appeal. It seemed he hadn't and the police had not traced the car. Bert thought about that. Maybe he couldn't own up to being there 'cos he was shagging someone's wife, or doing a big of burgling.

That afternoon Bert Smedley drove to Brightlingsea. The Volvo Estate was again parked on the forecourt in front of the solicitors' in the High Street. He drove past and parked his van further along the street, then walked back and inquired in the shop next door if they knew who owned the Volvo. He made the excuse he had a heavy load to deliver and wanted to put his van there.

'It belongs to one of the solicitors. Mr Labram,' they told him.

Bert returned to his van and chewed over the information. What was a solicitor doing sitting in his car outside someone's house in the middle of the night? Nothing respectable, he reckoned. More like something naughty.

Bert pondered some more. Entertaining Rene in a style to which he was unaccustomed in order to win her back was proving expensive. He badly needed more spending money and this could be his chance to lay his hands on some. He stepped down from the van and looked for a phone booth.

'There's a rough-sounding man on the phone who insists on speaking to you personally, Mr Labram,' Edgar Labram's secretary said apologetically.

'Put him on.'

Edgar Labram realized who the man was as soon as he spoke. Albert Smedley's voice matched his appearance.

Did Mr Labram know the police were trying to trace the driver of a silver Volvo Estate parked in Mile End Road the night a man called Dennison was murdered? the voice inquired.

'What has this to do with me?' Edgar Labram asked.

''Cos it was you, that's what.'

It wasn't his business, Bert Smedley went on, what Mr Labram was doing there in his car at that time of night, not his business at all. But since he hadn't come forward when the police appealed for him, what he'd been doing must have been naughty, something a respectable solicitor shouldn't be doing and wouldn't want his wife and friends to know about.

'Get to the point,' Labram growled.

'Point is, I reckon it's worth a bob or two to you to keep my mouth shut.'

'How much?' Labram snapped.

'I reckon five hundred quid 'ud be fair. An' listen . . . I won't be back for more. I'm not greedy.'

Edgar Labram made a pretence of agreeing, even feigning indignation. 'All right, but you'd damned well better *not* ask for more!' He knew where to find Albert Smedley and he had no intention of paying anything.

He listened to Bert Smedley's laborious explanation of how and where to hand over the money the following day, and hung up. From his desk drawer he took out the slip of paper on which he'd written the address of Albert Smedley, maker of fine furniture, and gazed at it, cogitating. Dealing with this oaf should be no problem after the successful way he'd disposed of Dennison and Marjorie Wilson.

Before closing the office, he unlocked his safe and took out the Smith and Wesson 38. Edgar had always wanted a gun and he'd readily accepted one when it was offered by one of his more dubious clients in payment of his fee. He caressed its dull black finish, savouring the feeling of power the weapon gave him.

After dinner that evening Edgar Labram drove to Halstead and located Smedley's isolated cottage. Leaving his car some distance away in the entrance to a field, he reconnoitred on foot.

The cottage was in darkness. At the rear, further along a path, Edgar saw light blazing from the window of a shed and headed towards it. Through the window he saw Smedley working. He watched him for a while, noting the various pieces of equipment in the shed and formulating a plan.

Smedley was taken by surprise. While he was bending over the sawbench guiding a length of rough-sawn oak through the electric saw, the motor suddenly died. He looked up and saw Edgar Labram with one hand on the switch and the other pointing a gun at him.

His jaw dropped. ''Ere, what d'you want? Who are you?'

'Oh, I think you can guess that.' Smiling maliciously, Edgar watched Smedley's eyes light up with fear.

113

'Look ... there ain't no need for this,' Smedley protested. 'I only—'

'Shut up!' Edgar snarled. 'Get up on the bench and lie on your back.' He waved the gun menacingly.

Smedley stared at the weapon, wondering if it was a replica and whether to risk making a grab at it. For no logical reason, he concluded that, being a solicitor's, the gun would be real. He scrambled onto the sawbench and lay down alongside the circular saw.

'No. Legs either side,' Edgar ordered.

Smedley's eyes rounded like saucers. ''Ere now, I ...'

'Do it!'

Smedley edged his body backwards until his head over-hung the end of the bench. Gingerly, he lifted a leg and placed it the other side of the circular saw, his crutch touching the teeth.

'Now what I want to know,' Edgar said in a coaxing tone of voice, his finger poised on the switch, 'is exactly what you've told the police.'

'I ain't told 'em nothing ... nothing at all. I swear.' Smedley was sweating heavily. 'An' I won't, neither. On me oath, I won't.'

'You've spoken to them, though?'

'Jess to check they was still interested in your car.'

'And were they?'

'Yeah.' Smedley was trembling violently. This man wasn't some philandering husband or Peeping Tom. More like he was the man who'd murdered Dennison. Mouth wobbling, he went on, 'It's OK, guv'nor, I didn't even give me name. I won't say a word, honest I won't.'

'No, I'm sure you won't.' Edgar Labram smiled malevolently.

Smedley's death would be accidental, he'd decided. From among the drilling, machining and sawing equip-ment in the shed, he'd chosen the electric saw as the lethal weapon. He would force Smedley at gunpoint to lay his arm across the sawbench. Then, a brief revolution of the saw which would slice into the flesh just deep enough to open an artery.

The scenario Edgar had in mind was of Smedley shaping a piece of wood . . . a moment of carelessness . . . the saw catching his arm and severing an artery. Blood gushing out . . . Smedley bleeding to death before he could reach the phone to summon help.

The plan was perfect, but there was something he had to make sure of first.

'I don't believe you didn't give the police your name. Why wouldn't you?' he asked.

'I daren't, see?' Smedley said earnestly. ' 'Cos they think I killed Dennison.'

'Why do they think that?'

'They said I done it 'cos he was having it off with me wife. It ain't true, but they had me in for questioning and gave me a right grilling.'

'Did they now?'

Edgar Labram digested the information. As he considered its implications he alighted on a much better way of disposing of Albert Smedley.

When Millson told Scobie Abigail Labram didn't know who raped her, Scobie thought that would be the end of the matter. Millson had other ideas, however, and Scobie felt near despair when he was asked to arrange another visit to Mrs Pennington.

'I can't believe she won't know – or at least have some idea,' Millson said.

It seemed to Scobie that George Millson had become obsessed with Abigail Labram and the past, and had lost sight of their present-day murder investigation. Scobie didn't believe there was any connection between events that happened a lifetime ago and the murders of John Dennison and Marjorie Wilson. He wished George would direct his energies to unearthing more evidence against Albert Smedley or looking for other suspects.

*　　　*　　　*

Peggy Pennington, wearing a print dress with a floral pattern, took them through into the conservatory again, after dispatching her husband to the kitchen to make tea.

'Tim's a nice man,' she explained, 'but he's a bit strait-laced and I don't think he'd like hearing about the things we got up to as teenagers. And that's what you've come to ask me about, isn't it?'

'More or less,' Millson said noncommittally.

'Well, before we start, Chief Inspector, I believe in plain speaking. Abby and Rachel have phoned me, so I know what's been happening and I don't like your tactics. However, I still have faith in the police, and I'm willing to believe you have good reasons for them, and know what you're doing.'

'I'm glad to hear it,' Millson said with mild sarcasm.

She acknowledged this with a wintry smile. 'So, what do you want to ask me?'

'Since you believe in plain speaking, Mrs Pennington, I want to know who raped your friend Abby.'

'She doesn't know. She told you so.'

'I'm asking *you*,' he said irritably. 'The rest of you must have talked it over between you and guessed who it was.'

'We didn't, as a matter of fact. You may find this hard to believe, but we never spoke about it again. It made it easier to put it out of our minds, you see. Chewing it over would have kept the whole ghastly business alive.'

'But you yourself must have some idea who the boy was.'

'It was fifty years ago,' she said tersely. 'He'd be old now.'

'Time doesn't alter the facts.'

'It alters one's perspective, though,' she said. 'We were very young . . . children by today's standards. Half the boys didn't know where to put it, if you'll forgive the crudeness. And some of us girls weren't much wiser.' Her expression relaxed in a faint smile. 'Though we knew that

116

much, of course. So it's really a question of who was capable of doing a thing like that.'

Her husband came through the glass doors carrying a tea tray. He placed it carefully on a cane table beside his wife.

'Thank you, Tim,' she said.

He nodded and walked on through the French windows and into the garden. She poured tea and handed cups to Millson and Scobie.

'Can you suggest some names?' Millson prompted, stirring his tea.

She turned her head, gazing down the garden into the distance. 'I did think about it at the time,' she admitted. She heaved a sigh. 'Very well. There were four who might have done it. Les Clare, Gordon Yemm, David Nelson and Arthur Turnbull, because he was older than the others. If I had to choose I'd say Gordon Yemm. He was a slimy little toad, always putting his hand up your skirt if you stood near his desk.'

'Do you know where they are now?' Scobie asked, writing down the names.

'Les Clare was killed in the war. I saw Arthur Turnbull at the reunion and I know David was invited, so presumably the new secretary has their addresses. I don't know what happened to Gordon Yemm. He didn't return to the office after the war.'

'Any idea who might know?' Scobie asked.

She pursed her lips. 'The Personnel Department perhaps. They keep staff records back to the year dot. Staff in the Forces were paid the difference between their civil pay and their Service pay, so Personnel had to keep track of them. You could start from there.'

She turned to Millson. 'Do you really believe one of these boys – well, he'd be my age now – killed Midge and John Dennison because they were blackmailing him?'

'I believe it's *possible*,' he corrected. 'Or if not him, then someone connected with him.'

*　　　*　　　*

Millson had a satisfied expression on his face as they drove away.

'Names at last,' he said.

Scobie nodded gloomily. Millson would follow this trail to the very end, tracking down and questioning three old men to find out if one of them was being blackmailed over a rape committed fifty years ago. It was bizarre. And they didn't know the whereabouts of one of them, or if he was even alive.

He opened his case and took out Kenneth Clark's list. 'David Nelson's address is here,' he informed Millson, scanning the pages, 'but Arthur Turnbull isn't on the list.'

'He should be. Mrs Pennington said he was at the reunion. Give Clark a ring when we get back. And ask him about Yemm too. He's the one to go for first, from what Mrs Pennington said.'

'Clark left Turnbull's name off the list because he's dead,' Scobie informed Millson next day. 'He died last January.'

'That rules him out, then,' Millson said. 'You can't blackmail a dead man. And Yemm?'

'Clark has never heard of him. I tried Personnel. They're ringing me back.'

At first, the Staff Records section in the Personnel Department had refused even to confirm that Gordon Yemm had once served in the department. For security reasons, a clerk explained, it was not their policy to answer questions about past or present staff employed by the department, or to give their whereabouts.

'This is a murder investigation,' Scobie said.

He was transferred to the head of section, who was not impressed and told him the department would only provide information in the case of a definite suspect against whom the police had evidence.

'He is and we have,' Scobie said firmly, certain it was what Millson would have said.

It transpired there was no Gordon Yemm on either the active or retired list of staff and the archive files would have to be called for. These were kept at Boreham Wood and it would take a while to search through them.

Two days later a clerk phoned Scobie and reported that Gordon Yemm had joined the Home Office as a clerical officer in 1939 and been evacuated to Bournemouth in 1940. He'd been called up the following April and served in the army until demobilization in 1946.

'He returned to the department for a few months and then resigned,' the clerk said. 'There's no later information on him.'

'Last known location?' Scobie inquired.

'An address on the Isle of Dogs. It doesn't exist now. It was in the Docklands development area.'

Scobie put down the phone and went into the incident room. It had been scaled down and some of the staff returned to other duties now the nationwide inquiries had ended. If Yemm was alive there was a fair chance he owned a car. Scobie sat down at a terminal and interrogated the Vehicle Owners Index on the Police National Computer.

Gordon Yemm was the registered keeper of a Vauxhall Cavalier and lived at Primrose Cottage, Ridgewell.

CHAPTER 14

Primrose Cottage was one of a cluster of dwellings on the A604 just outside the village of Ridgewell. The cottage lay back from the road behind a ten-foot-high hedge of Leylandii.

An elderly, bald man answered the door. 'Mr Yemm?' Millson asked.

'No, I'm Hedley Harman. Who wants him?'

'We're police officers. Is he in?'

'Yes.' He called over his shoulder. 'Gordon?'

A short man, also elderly, with grey hair and prominent teeth came to the door. 'What is it?' The teeth protruded and when he spoke his lips peeled back from them like a monkey's.

Millson showed his warrant card. 'I'm DCI Millson and this is DS Scobie. May we come in?'

'Yes, sure.'

Gordon Yemm led them into a sitting room. An upright piano stood against a wall and beside it was a stool with a low music stand in front of it.

'What's this about?' Yemm asked as they took seats.

Millson glanced pointedly at Hedley Harman who had followed them in and sat down next to Yemm.

'Hedley and I don't have any secrets from each other,' Yemm said.

Millson shrugged. 'As you wish. We're investigating the murder of a Mr John Dennison.'

'Oh, him. Yes, I read about the case.'

'Did you know him?'

'No, though he called on us about a year ago. Goodness

knows how he traced us. It was about some reunion of evacuees he'd been asked to organize by the Home Office Retired Staff Association. We were both evacuated to Bournemouth in 1940, you see. We said we couldn't face meeting people we hadn't seen for fifty years.' Yemm grimaced. 'I mean, think what they'd all look like now.'

The two men exchanged smiles. Scobie tried to interpret their expressions. Two old men living together for convenience and companionship? Or was the relationship closer than that?

Millson said, 'I'd like to ask you about the time you were in Bournemouth. You were billeted at a guesthouse called Larnaca, I believe.'

They both looked astonished. 'Yes, that's right,' said Yemm. 'Hedley and I shared a bedroom with two other lads.'

'And do you remember a party there at Christmas?'

'Not half,' said Harman. 'Wild . . . real wild, it was.'

'We provided the music,' Yemm said. 'Hedley played the piano. I played sax and clarinet.'

'They called him Gobstick Gordon,' Harman said with a laugh. Yemm's face opened in a monkey grin.

'There was a game last thing that night called "Goodnight Sweetheart",' Millson said.

'That's right. Fancy you knowing that,' Yemm said.

'Did you know a girl was raped during the game?'

'Only one?' Harman asked with a laugh. 'More likely she changed her mind. Was it Chrissy Campbell? Chrissy screamed rape if you even touched her.'

Millson said sharply, 'This isn't funny!'

'Oh, give over, Chief Inspector,' said Yemm. 'We were all as randy as hell in those days and the girls were worse than the fellows. It couldn't have been serious or we'd have heard about it.'

Millson glowered at him. 'It *was* serious. Very serious. The girl was too upset to report it.'

'Oh . . . sorry.' Yemm looked contrite. 'Who was the girl?'

'Abigail,' Millson said, and saw a fleeting change of expression in Yemm's eyes.

Harman said, 'Abby Coran? What a shame. She was a little sweetie.'

'What's all this to do with me?' Yemm asked.

'We believe the man concerned is now being black-mailed about the affair,' said Millson, watching his face. Again there was a reaction he couldn't identify.

'I still don't understand why you're questioning me,' he said.

'In order to eliminate you from our inquiries,' Millson explained. 'You were there that night.'

'Along with me and twenty other boys,' Hedley Harman said tersely.

He rose and stood behind Yemm's chair, laying a hand on his shoulder. Yemm reached up and patted Harman's hand.

Peggy Pennington must be mistaken about Yemm, Scobie thought. Or he could have changed, of course. You could never tell how people would turn out.

'Do you mind telling me where you were the night John Dennison was murdered, Mr Yemm? Thursday, March 28th.'

Yemm glanced at Hedley Harman who took out a pocket diary and flicked the pages. 'We were at the village hall in Yeldham playing Forties' dance music for the Senior Citizens' Club,' Harman said. 'We're always there on the last Thursday of the month. We have our own band, you know, the Blue Revellers.'

He noticed Scobie writing it down and said crossly, 'We don't know anything about the murder of Mr Dennison or about any rape.' He threw himself into his chair and folded his arms.

Millson turned to Yemm. 'You reacted just now when I told you the girl was Abigail. Why was that?'

'I was shocked.'

'Do you know which boy it was?'

Yemm goggled at him. 'No, doesn't Abby know?'

'No, it took place in total darkness. Were there any rumours at the time? Any talk among the lads?'

'I didn't hear any.'

'So, you've absolutely no idea?'

'No.'

Millson turned to Harman. 'And you?'

Harman glanced at Yemm, then shrugged and shook his head.

'What about David Nelson?' Scobie asked.

'Shouldn't think so,' Harman said. 'He was a decent lad.'

Millson was depressed on the drive back from Ridgewell. Scobie wasn't surprised and felt little sympathy. He'd always believed this trail would lead them into the sand. To his amazement though, Millson wasn't abandoning the hunt.

'Fix up to see David Nelson, as soon as possible, Norris,' he said.

In Primrose Cottage, Hedley Harman finished pouring coffee and handed the cup to Gordon Yemm.

'We should have told them, Gordon.'

Yemm heaped a spoonful of sugar into his coffee and stirred it. 'No, we shouldn't. The man's dead, for God's sake.'

That afternoon, Irene Smedley reported her husband missing.

'She hasn't seen him for several days,' Scobie told Millson.

'Lucky her.'

'She says they were getting together again and she's convinced something's happened to him.'

Millson waved his hand dismissively. 'List him as a missing person.'

'He's a suspect,' Scobie protested, 'and he's done a runner.' In Scobie's opinion it was Smedley who had murdered John Dennison, not some hypothetical black-mail victim.

'There's no evidence he's done a runner, as you put it, Norris. He's probably gone off on a drinking binge.' Millson saw Scobie's mouth set obstinately and waved his hand again. 'All right, put out an alert for him.'

David Nelson lived in a studio flat at the top of a five-storey house that backed onto Hampstead Heath. Millson buzzed the entry phone and he and Scobie climbed the flights of stairs. They were both panting when they reached the top.

Nelson was a tall man, with a slight stoop and thinning white hair. He greeted them courteously in a deep baritone voice that emanated warmth and kindness. The man should have been a clergyman, Scobie thought.

'Don't mind, do you?' Nelson waved a pipe at them. 'Not many of us pipe smokers left these days.'

'Not at all.' Millson pulled out his cigarettes.

Scobie waved a hand in assent and resigned himself to being kippered in the small room.

They sat down and David Nelson began cramming tobacco into the bowl of the pipe. 'How can I help you, Chief Inspector? I saw you at Midge's funeral. Is this visit to do with her suicide?'

'In a way,' Millson said cautiously, not intending to enlighten him on Marjorie Wilson's death. 'How well did you know her?'

'Oh, very well . . . once. That was a long time ago, though.'

'Would that be in 1940?'

'Yes, as a matter of fact it was.' David Nelson struck a match and put it to the bowl of the pipe, his mouth sucking the stem. After several puffs, he removed the stem from his mouth and said, 'I couldn't believe it when she killed herself. I thought I'd made things all right for her.'

Millson frowned. 'Would you mind explaining that remark, please?'

'Um . . .' David Nelson hesitated and looked embarrassed. 'Well, you see, I fell in love with Midge when I was eighteen and although the war parted us, and we never met again, I . . .' He paused.

Scobie glanced up from making notes and was astonished to see the elderly David Nelson blushing like a schoolboy.

'I know this sounds silly,' Nelson continued, 'but I went on loving her . . . loving the memory really, I suppose. When Betty Foster told me in one of her letters that Midge was living in poverty and would have to give up her home because she couldn't keep up the mortgage repayments I . . . well, I just couldn't bear the thought of it. Midge had been such a cheerful, determined girl. It was a dreadful thing to happen to her. I got Betty to find out where Midge banked and paid in a fairly large credit to her account to help her out. Anonymously, of course. It was no hardship for me – I'm quite comfortable financially.' He sighed. 'But it seems it was no good.'

Scobie stole a glance at Millson's face. He recognized the expression on it. Inside, Millson was hurting.

Millson asked woodenly, 'How much was the credit, Mr Nelson?'

'Five thousand pounds.'

Millson nodded. With three words this romantic old man had shattered the blackmail evidence against Marjorie Wilson.

He asked a last question out of curiosity. 'Why didn't you go to the reunion, Mr Nelson?'

'Old memories of moments of delight are very fragile, Chief Inspector. I don't think mine would have survived a face-to-face contact fifty years on.'

Millson was silent and morose as they drove back to Colchester, smoking cigarette after cigarette. Scobie, who was driving, surreptitiously edged his window open and directed the air vent in the facia onto his face.

Millson eventually broke his silence at Marks Tey. As the A12 dual carriageway widened into four lanes and

Scobie accelerated to overtake a string of lorries, he said gloomily, 'I'm at a dead end, Norris. I don't know who raped Abigail Labram. I don't know if Marjorie Wilson's death was unconnected with Dennison's, or her killer made the same assumption as we did about that five thousand pounds. And now Smedley's taken off into the blue, I'm not even sure Dennison *was* killed by one of his blackmail victims. In short, Norris, I know sweet FA,' he added bitterly. 'And I don't know where to go from here.'

Scobie glanced sideways at him. He hadn't seen Millson look so dejected for a long time. 'Something will turn up, George,' he said comfortingly.

Something did, and it provided a target for Millson's anger and frustration.

'What d'you mean, it was overlooked?' he bawled half an hour later at an apologetic DC in the incident room.

'I didn't think it was important, sir.' The DC still didn't think so. He'd only belatedly reported the brief phone call as a matter of routine.

'What did the man say?' Millson thundered, glaring at him.

'He asked if we still wanted to know about the car across the street the night Dennison was murdered.'

'And?'

'I told him we did.'

'And?' Millson repeated impatiently.

'It's all on tape, sir.'

'Well, let's hear it then.'

The DC scuttled away and retrieved the tape and a recorder from a cabinet. 'It's not much, sir,' he said nervously as he loaded the cassette into the machine and pressed the play button.

Millson and Scobie listened to the playback.

'Your name, please?'

'I told you . . . I ain't giving it. D'you wanna know or not?'

'Yes, we do.'

There was a click, followed by the dialling tone.

'Is that it?' Millson demanded.

126

'Yes, sir.' The DC waited for the storm to break around his head.

He was saved by Scobie saying, 'Hang on. Play it again.'

The DC pressed the rewind button briefly and the tape replayed.

'That's Smedley's voice,' Scobie said.

'Are you sure?' Millson asked.

'Certain.'

Millson rubbed his chin. 'So, Smedley rings to check that we don't know something he does . . . and a couple of days later he's missing.' He swung round to Scobie. 'Dig out the statement he made when we had him in for questioning.'

In Millson's office ten minutes later, Scobie paraphrased Smedley's words. 'He was hanging around the house from half twelve to one o'clock . . . saw a man in a car watching the house . . . light-coloured, possibly silver, Volvo Estate . . . couldn't see his face or describe him.'

Millson smiled wolfishly. 'I think his wife's right to be worried. My guess is he discovered whose car it was, checked the man hadn't answered our appeal and we don't know who he is, then put the bite on him.'

Millson reached for his coat. 'We'll take a run out to his place and pay Mrs Smedley a call on the way.'

CHAPTER 15

Irene Smedley had just arrived home from work when they called and was dressed in her shop assistant's outfit of black skirt and white blouse. She looked a different woman to the one they had interviewed three months ago, except that she had the habitual small cigar between her fingers when she opened the door to them. Millson explained they were looking into her husband's disappearance.

'You took your time,' she complained as she led them into the sitting room and they sat down. 'I reported him missing two days ago.'

'We only deal urgently with missing person reports if a child is involved or we have reason to believe a crime has been committed,' Millson replied. 'When did you last see your husband?'

'A week ago today. We went for a drink in the Bull at Halstead.'

'I thought you and your husband didn't get on?'

'We didn't. But he's changed. He wants us to try and make a go of things. I told him I needed time to get used to the idea.' She grinned. 'He's sort of courting me again.'

'So he wouldn't have gone off with someone else?' Scobie asked.

'Not the way he's been chasing after me,' she said with a smirk. 'Something's happened to him. I've rung the hospitals and I've been out to his place. The doors are unlocked and his van's still there. Bert wouldn't leave the place like that.' She drew on the cigar and puffed out smoke. 'I locked up and brought away the keys. And I left a note on the door in case he came back.'

'Did you notice anything unusual or suspicious while you were there?' Millson asked.

She shook her head.

'Did you search the grounds?'

'No.' Her hand went to her mouth. 'You don't think he was lying there somewhere, do you? Had a heart attack, p'raps?'

A heart attack wasn't the demise Millson had in mind, but he said soothingly, 'Could be. Don't start worrying yet, though. We're on our way there now and we'll have a good look round for him.'

'Oh, thanks.' She smiled ruefully. 'He wasn't that bad, you know. I was just getting to like him again.'

Millson nodded sympathetically. 'When you last spoke, did he mention meeting anyone, or going away?'

'The only going away Bert was planning was a dirty weekend with me.' She laughed deep in her throat. 'I said I'd think about it.'

Scobie asked her, 'Do you have a photograph of your husband, Mrs Smedley?'

'Yeah, sure.'

Grinding the stub of the cigar in an ashtray, she stood up and lifted an album of photographs down from a bookshelf. She opened it and flipped through the plastic holders inside. She stopped at one of them and extracted the photograph from it.

'This was taken on holiday in Great Yarmouth. He looks a bit older now. Will that do?' she asked, holding it out to Scobie. 'He's got no clothes on.'

Scobie peered at a hairy-chested Bert Smedley in bathing trunks. He nodded and took the photograph from her. 'We'll only use the face,' he said.

'And may we borrow his keys, please?' Millson asked.

'Yeah, OK.' She replaced the album and went to her handbag on the sideboard. 'What d'you think's happened to him, Mr Millson?' she asked, handing him the keys.

'That's what we'll try to find out,' Millson promised.

Irene Smedley's note was still pinned to the front door when Millson and Scobie tramped up the track to the cottage. In the kitchen there was a dirty plate and cutlery in the sink.

'Last meal he had was supper, by the looks of it,' Millson said, peering at the remains of food on the plate.

They spent half an hour searching the cottage, the shed and the grounds, and found nothing untoward. There was no Albert Smedley and no sign of blood or violence. And his Toyota van was parked alongside the shed.

'He must have left in someone else's vehicle,' Scobie said.

Millson nodded. 'Either that or his body's around here somewhere.'

His eyes roamed the surrounding fields and woods. 'We need a search party up here first thing tomorrow.'

Next morning copies of a head-and-shoulders picture of Albert Smedley were issued to the media with an appeal for information on his whereabouts. Uniformed police began searching the area around his cottage and detectives visited nearby farms and houses to ask what vehicles and callers had been seen at the cottage in the last seven days.

Millson also set another line of inquiry in motion. 'If Smedley was telling us the truth about a man watching Dennison's house, he could be the murderer,' he told his team. 'We have to find him if only to eliminate him. I want a fresh appeal put out for him to come forward and another house-to-house inquiry in Mile End Road. In particular, I want the two witnesses who thought they saw him questioned again.'

Edgar Labram studied his secretary covertly as he dictated letters to her. It wasn't easy to find a suitable companion at his age. He'd tried a marriage bureau last year and been offered a string of divorcees eager to remarry and lonely widows lying about their age. He needed someone whose background he knew. A woman he could trust.

Tracey had joined the firm two years ago after her boyfriend walked out on her. She was thirty-five, attractive, and she seemed docile and pliable. Moreover, she'd been very sympathetic over his divorce and he was certain she liked him. Tracey would do nicely, Edgar felt. He'd find an excuse to invite her to dinner at Spencers to give her an eyeful of his future prospects, as it were, and see how she reacted.

He finished dictating and dismissed her with a smile. Folding his hands across his paunch, he relaxed in pleasant contemplation of his future. It was unclouded now that he'd killed Dennison's accomplice and dealt with that thug, Smedley. His method of disposing of Smedley had been a masterstroke.

Edgar smiled sardonically. He'd made a rapid change of plan when he learned the police suspected Smedley of murdering Dennison. He'd decided to add to their suspicions by making Smedley disappear.

Late that night he drove to Sudbury. He knew the area well from the time he lived there with his wife before their divorce. On the outskirts of the town the district council provided the citizens with a household waste site equipped with the latest machines for the disposal of refuse. The site was isolated – the local residents objected to having a waste site near their homes – and screened by trees at the end of a country lane that led nowhere.

Townspeople used it for the disposal of junk that wouldn't go in their Wheelie bins, like old chairs, televisions and fridges. The items had to be carried up concrete steps and dropped into a rectangular hopper six feet deep and four feet wide. The hopper was enclosed on three sides by a steel hood and was attached to the side of a container the size of a small garage.

When the hopper became full an attendant closed the lid and switched on the power. Inside the hopper, a piston moved forward and back, the walls advanced and receded, and the rubbish was compacted into a rectangular block and ejected into the large container.

When the container itself was full it was craned onto a lorry and taken away to be emptied into a barge. The barge was towed out to sea where its bowels opened and disgorged the rubbish into the North Sea.

Edgar Labram drove quietly into the compound of the waste site and parked beside one of the machines. Albert Smedley lay in the rear of the Estate covered with a blanket, his hands tied behind his back.

Edgar turned off the engine. Taking a torch and screwdriver from the car, he walked across to the hut at the side of the compound where the key to the switchgear was kept. He prised open the casement window and climbed inside.

Returning with the key, he stood by the car looking around and listening. The night was silent and the nearest habitation, a row of bungalows, was half a mile away. He opened the tailgate of the Estate, hauled Smedley out and guided him in the darkness up the concrete steps to the hopper. A confused Smedley peered around him with no idea of where he was.

The safety gate was waist high, designed to prevent people falling in accidentally as they hurled in their lumber. Edgar Labram pushed Smedley forward and bent him double over the parapet. Stooping, he seized his ankles and heaved him into the hopper, quickly closing the steel lid to cut off his cursing and shouting in the bottom of the hopper.

Stepping down, he inserted the safety key into the motor and turned the switch. There was a rumbling sound as the hydraulic piston rammed forward in the first part of the crushing process. Smedley screamed twice, the sound barely carrying above the whir of machinery, before the walls moved in and his pulped body was enfolded with the crushed remains of a freezer and gas stove that had been thrown in earlier that day.

The compacted rectangle was ejected into the large container and the cycle of movements ended. Edgar switched off the machine, opened the guard door of the hopper and shone his torch down inside. The light reflected on clean, shining steel. Removing the key from the switch, he returned it to the hut and got into his car.

Silence closed in on the waste site again as the Volvo slid out of the compound and the sound of its engine died away towards Sudbury.

After two days, the police search around Albert Smedley's cottage was called off. Nothing useful had been found and there was no indication of what had happened to him. The local inquiries also produced no leads. There had been no strangers seen in the area recently, and no one had noticed any callers or vehicles at the cottage.

By the end of a week the publication of Smedley's photograph had produced reported sightings of him from all over the country. Millson was pessimistic about them.

'If we issued a picture of my grandfather some people would swear they'd seen him somewhere or other yesterday. And he's been dead twenty years. I doubt if any of these reports relate to Smedley.'

The result of the second round of house-to-house inquiries in Mile End Road was more promising. Two residents now said they had seen a Volvo Estate parked in the street opposite Dennison's flat on the night of the murder. One had noticed it around eleven o'clock. The other, a milkman, was sure he'd seen a man sitting in it just before he set off for work at his depot at two o'clock in the morning.

'That puts him there at the time of the murder,' Millson said as he discussed the reports with Scobie. 'Dennison was killed between midnight and 3.00 a.m. according to the PM report. I think this is our man, Norris.'

'Why did he sit there for three hours, though?'

Millson's eyes crinkled at the corners. 'Dennison was downstairs humping Irene Smedley until one o'clock, if you remember. Our man had to wait for him to go to bed in his own flat before he could break in and kill him.'

Edgar Labram glanced at the clock. Nearly time for him to step across the road for lunch at his usual restaurant. He stood up from his desk and looked out of the window at the bright June sunshine. Tracey was out shopping. When she returned he would invite her to dinner at Spencers.

He stretched luxuriously, a smile hovering round his lips. She'd become aware of his interest in her and had begun giving him little smiles and standing close to him when she brought work to his desk.

The phone rang. He stepped to his desk and picked it up. 'Yes?'

'Are you alone?' The hairs rose on the back of Edgar's neck. It was the same synthesized voice. *You're dead*! *I killed you*! he wanted to shout down the phone.

'Hullo? Are you there?' the voice called when he didn't answer.

Edgar struggled to control his panic. 'Yes, I'm here,' he said.

'I want another five thousand. The same arrangement as before. Tomorrow at twelve.'

'No, wait! Wait!' he said desperately. 'I can't. I don't have that amount of money to hand and it's impossible to get it by tomorrow.'

The last payment had drained his current account and the rest of his private money was in a building society account that required notice to be given of large withdrawals. And he couldn't make a withdrawal from the firm's account without a countersignature by his partner, Caldwell, who was a stickler for checking and counterchecking every payment.

He gabbled an explanation down the phone. There was a brief silence on the other end of the line. Then, 'Make the withdrawal,' the voice said. 'You'll be contacted again a week today.'

Edgar replaced the phone with trembling hands. Killing Marjorie Wilson had achieved nothing. She hadn't been Dennison's accomplice, someone else had, and these demands would go on and on, draining his assets away.

He sat down at his desk and put his head in his hands. He had to find out who the blackmailer was and kill him . . . or her. There could be no rosy future with Tracey until he did.

When Millson returned from lunch at the Red Lion, Gordon Yemm was waiting to see him.

'Hedley made me come and see you, Chief Inspector. I don't think it's important, but he won't stop nagging me until I tell you.'

'Tell me what?' Millson asked.

'That it was probably Arthur Turnbull who raped Abby.'

'He's dead,' Millson said.

'I know. And that's what I told Hedley, but he still wanted me to tell you.'

'Why do you think it was Turnbull?'

'Well, about a week before the party, Arthur had a fight with Mike Labram. Over a girl. We used to call Arthur the blond beast. He was older than the rest of us and thought he could do what he liked with a girl. Anyway, the point is, Mike gave Arthur a drubbing and made him look a fool in front of everyone. Then at the party, you could see Mike and Abby were taken with each other and Arthur was jealous. He couldn't take his eyes off Abby. And while Hedley and I were having a break from playing the music, we heard Arthur bragging to one of his cronies he was going to have Abby before Mike did. That's what he said and that's what Hedley wanted me to tell you. We're pretty sure it was Arthur did that to Abby.'

It was a letter from the Inland Revenue the following morning that prompted Edgar Labram to consider his ex-wife as the blackmailer. She was still arguing about her

135

tax liability from two years ago, before they were divorced, and the Revenue had agreed to apportion more of the liability to him.

Edgar read the letter and sneered. Typical of Val . . . wanting every penny. Like a key turning in a lock, the words 'every penny' opened a memory. Of Val screaming down the phone at him when she discovered he was contesting her claim for a share of the house: 'You won't get away with this! I'll screw you and your family for every penny!'

In the event, he had got away with it. He'd remortgaged the house before the divorce proceedings began, and left her with a debt. Val had raged and stormed, but there was nothing she could do about it.

Recalling her fury, Edgar began to see his ex-wife in a new light. Until now, he'd been so sure the blackmailer was someone from his mother's past he hadn't considered a present-day enemy.

He and Val had often spent weekends and holidays at Spencers before their marriage broke up. Suppose Val had snooped around and come across some document or letters his mother kept that showed he wasn't Mike Labram's son? She wouldn't let on to him because that would have given her away. Then, when she found he'd tricked her over the divorce, used her knowledge to blackmail first his mother and then him.

Also she had been at Spencers last summer when Dennison called to see Mike about the reunion. Mike didn't approve of divorce and had invited her there to discuss a reconciliation. Val would have none of it, of course. After tea, Dennison had given her a lift to the station in his car.

Edgar's face darkened. Well, if it was Valerie who had her claws into him, he knew how to deal with her.

CHAPTER 16

At home that evening George Millson served Italian pancakes for the evening meal, to be washed down with a bottle of Buzet Dena had bought for his birthday last month.

'It was very expensive, I hope you like it,' she said, as he brought it to the table.

He read the label. It was a numbered bottle. 'I'm impressed,' he said. 'Thank you.' He poured himself a glass.

'Is this a celebration then?' Dena asked.

'No. I just felt like having a nice meal this evening.'

'I thought so,' she said knowingly. 'You always stuff yourself when you're doing badly on a case.'

'Don't be cheeky,' he said sharply. 'Or you'll get beans on toast for the rest of the week.'

'Ugh. Can I try some wine?'

Millson hesitated. Why not? The French gave their children wine. Diluted with water. He wasn't going to ruin a good wine in that way. He poured a quarter glass and handed it to her.

She took a sip and made a face. 'I don't know why you like it.'

Perhaps he should have diluted it after all. 'It's an acquired taste,' he said.

'Julie says wine's for oldies. She says rum and coke's nice.'

Julie would, he thought moodily.

After dinner, Dena loaded the dishwasher and disappeared upstairs to play her latest CD. Millson subsided into an armchair to dispose of the rest of the Buzet.

137

Relaxed and pleasantly languid, he began reviewing his investigation. Dena was right, it was not going well. All he had were unconnected bits of information like the pieces of a jigsaw, and he couldn't fit them together to make a picture. If it was Arthur Turnbull who raped Abby, he couldn't be Dennison's blackmail victim because he was dead. Or was he being blackmailed before then? Perhaps he'd been driven to his death by the worry and someone in his family had taken revenge. Was that who the man in the Volvo was, a relative? Tenuous.

The coincidence of Abigail Labram handing over money to Dennison the very night he was murdered continued to bother Millson. The money that hadn't been found. He'd thought it possible Sarah Howarth was at the Oak Tree and Dennison had passed the money to her. The re-examination he'd ordered of witness statements hadn't turned up a girl that fitted her description though.

Scobie accused him of being hooked on the past, looking backwards instead of forwards. Maybe. He began mulling over the information. Information from Peggy Pennington . . . Rachel . . . Yemm. He closed his eyes, visualizing those scenes in the past. They were like scenes from an old silent film. The dark-haired maiden, Abby . . . the blond hero, Mike . . . and the villain, Arthur Turnbull.

George Millson's mind was far away, preoccupied with images, when Dena came down in her pyjamas to say goodnight. As she bent to kiss him her hair brushed across his cheek. The hair was dark like his own, except it was long and his was short. Her movement intruded on his daydreaming and suddenly his eyes snapped open and his face froze into a mask.

Dena straightened and stared at him. 'What did I do? You look gobsmacked.'

'You've just solved a riddle for me,' he said, his face mobile again.

'Do I get a reward?'

'Yep. I'll do breakfast tomorrow.' The usual arrangement was that Dena prepared breakfast and he cooked dinner.

'Oh, good.' She shuffled off in her slippers to bed.

'Why are we seeing Abigail Labram again?' Scobie asked next morning as he stepped into Millson's car.

'Last night, I realized we'd overlooked a slip she made in one of the stories she told us. I want to confirm it.'

'Are you going to tell me what it is?'

'No.'

'Not even a clue?' Scobie pressed.

'All right.' Millson smiled crookedly. ' "Like father, like son." Try it the other way round.'

Scobie was still puzzling it out as they were shown into the drawing room at Spencers. Abigail Labram stood in the centre of the room, head held high.

'What is it this time, Chief Inspector?' There was a tremor of anxiety in her voice.

Scobie moved discreetly to the side of the room. Millson had told him not to take notes.

'First, an apology, Mrs Labram,' Millson said. 'I was wrong about your friend Midge Wilson. She had nothing to do with your blackmail.'

'Oh . . . that.' She shrugged. 'I knew it wasn't true. But thank you for apologizing.'

Millson stepped forward and lifted down the photograph of Abigail and her husband and son from the mantelpiece.

'Edgar and your husband are quite a bit alike,' he commented.

'You mean, since they're not father and son?' There was an edge to her voice.

He nodded. 'Fortunate too, considering your son was the result of some casual liaison with an Australian airman.' He turned and faced her. 'Though that wasn't true, was it, Mrs Labram?'

She frowned. 'Yes, of course it was! Why would I lie about a thing like that?'

'Because the truth is rather worse,' he said.

She made a quick movement of her head. 'Reared up like a startled fawn,' as Scobie described it to Millson later.

'I don't know what you mean.' Her voice was tense.

'You told us this Australian had dark, curly hair. That was your description, I recall. Dark hair,' he repeated.

'What does it matter, for heaven's sake, whether Edgar's father was dark or fair?'

Scobie suddenly grasped the meaning of Millson's clue and understood where his questions were leading.

'It matters,' Millson said, pointing to the photograph, 'because you had dark hair and if Edgar's father was dark the probability is that Edgar would have dark hair too.'

Her eyes widened. 'Please stop this!' she said desperately.

Millson knew from her reaction he was right and there had been a tragic consequence for Abigail after that fateful Christmas party. He closed his mind against her pleading expression. The words had to be said and she would never say them herself.

He said gently, 'It was the rape that made you pregnant, not some stray airman. The boy who did that to you was fair-haired and his name was Arthur Turnbull.'

Her eyes had grown enormous. Blindly, she reached for the nearest chair and sank down on it. After a moment, head bowed, she said in a whisper so that he could hardly catch her words, 'Yes, that's how Edgar was conceived. Arthur is his real father.' Her body convulsed in a shudder. 'He was a horrible person. Mike loathed him.' She raised her head. 'Do you have a cigarette, please?'

'Yes, of course.' He dived in his pocket.

After he'd lit the cigarette for her, she went on. 'Abortion wasn't an option in those days and I did the only thing I could. I married Mike and let him think the child was his.' She looked at Millson defiantly. 'I loved him anyway . . . and we've been very happy.'

Millson nodded sympathetically. 'I'm sure you have.'

She drew on the cigarette, blowing out smoke through

140

her nostrils. 'All my life I've tried not to see Arthur Turnbull in Edgar. But . . . sometimes . . .' She shook her head miserably. 'If only he'd been Mike's son.'

She smoked for a while in silence, lost in thought. Eventually she said, 'I don't see what use it is to you knowing about Arthur Turnbull.'

'It's possible he was being blackmailed by Dennison over what he did to you.'

'But Arthur's dead. Midge told me.'

'I know. He died in January.'

'January? You mean before—?' She broke off. 'I thought . . .' She stopped again, looking puzzled.

'You thought what, Mrs Labram?' Millson asked.

'I thought it was Arthur who was blackmailing me. It would be the sort of thing he would do if he found out. Midge didn't say when he died, just that it was recently. I thought that's why I didn't hear any more and why he couldn't be Mr Dennison's other victim.'

'The blackmail could have started before he died,' Millson said.

'I can't see Arthur worrying about what he did to me fifty years ago. He'd just laugh about it.'

'He might worry if he had a family he cared about. A threat to tell them he was a rapist would be pretty effective.'

'But if he died in January, he can't have killed Mr Dennison.'

'Someone in his family could have, though, in revenge for destroying their lives,' Millson said.

'Yes, I suppose so.' Her face clouded. 'Our lives would be destroyed too if my husband and son learned the truth,' she said.

'They won't hear it from us,' Millson said. He held out his hand. 'This has been a distressing interview for you, Mrs Labram, and I'm very grateful for your help.'

She accompanied them into the hall. As they emerged from the drawing room a pair of feet racing up the curving staircase disappeared from sight onto the landing. Worried

141

by yet another visit from the police, Edgar Labram had been attempting to eavesdrop at the drawing-room door.

Crossing the hall, Abigail Labram asked, 'Could it be one of Arthur Turnbull's family who was blackmailing me, Chief Inspector?'

'It's possible,' Millson said, 'except it wouldn't explain John Dennison's murder.'

On the landing, Edgar Labram heard the exchange and attached no significance to it. The police obviously weren't making any progress on the murder and that was all he was concerned with.

'Mendel's Law,' Scobie muttered as they drove away. 'I should have remembered.'

Millson frowned. 'What?'

'That's what you meant by "Like father like son", wasn't it?'

'No.'

'How did you work it out then?'

'From my daughter's hair,' Millson said. 'Being the same as mine, I mean. That and the photo on the mantelpiece. Abigail had dark hair when she was young and Edgar's was fair, like Michael Labram's. I remembered she'd told us his real father had dark hair and it set me wondering. I cast my mind over all the parents I'd met at Dena's school . . . and their daughters . . . and couldn't recall a single girl with fair hair whose mother and father were both dark.'

'There should be one or two among them,' Scobie said. 'The chances are one in sixteen.'

'Well, I didn't meet any and it convinced me Abigail Labram invented the story about the Aussie airman to avoid telling us how Edgar was really conceived. Yemm was sure it was Turnbull who raped Abigail, and described him as a blond beast. The answer was obvious.'

'So, you don't even know Mendel's theory of dominant and recessive genes?'

142

Millson waved his hand airily. 'I've heard of it. But I couldn't explain it for the life of me.'

Scobie refrained from comment, exasperated that Millson had arrived at the right conclusion from such crude reasoning.

'What now?' he asked after a while.

'Ask Kenneth Clark for Arthur Turnbull's address when he died, then go see what we can find out.'

Valerie Labram slipped off her clothes and stepped into the bath. The water was lukewarm, not hot as she would have liked it, but she had to economize. It was humiliating having to struggle with bills at her age. Aggravating too, since it wasn't her fault she was short of money. She should have been comfortably off with her half-share of the house when she divorced Edgar.

Valerie had wanted to divorce her husband on grounds of cruelty. She had plenty of evidence. Her solicitor, however, persuaded her to plead 'irreparable breakdown of the marriage', pointing out that Edgar was bound to defend a cruelty suit, and she was unlikely to win against a husband who was a solicitor. Valerie believed the truth was that he objected to proceeding against a fellow solicitor.

She had continued working as Edgar's secretary when they were married, and after twenty years of marriage she considered herself entitled to a substantial share of their house in Sudbury. She asked for – and was granted – half the value of the house in the divorce settlement. What she then discovered, though, was that a document Edgar had asked her to sign the year before had enabled him to increase their joint mortgage. He had mortgaged the property to the hilt and put the money into his practice. Worse still, with the recession in the housing market, the house was worth less than the mortgage and she was left with nothing. Or, as an estate agent described it to her, half of a negative equity.

When Valerie realized Edgar had defrauded her of her share of the house and that at the age of forty-eight she would have to start work again to keep a roof over her head, she promised herself revenge.

Valerie climbed out of the bath, dried herself and put on a bathrobe. She went down to the kitchen to prepare her evening meal and was about to turn on the oven when the doorbell rang.

When she opened the door, her ex-husband was standing on the step. 'What are you doing here?' she demanded.

'I was passing through and thought I'd drop in to see how you were.'

'You what?' she asked incredulously.

'I wondered if you were all right for money.'

'Money!' She spat the word at him. 'You know damned well I'm not, you thieving skunk!'

'Don't be like that, Val. I was strapped for cash at the time and I had to think of the business.'

Edgar gave her an ingratiating smile. The strategy he'd settled upon involved being pleasant to his ex-wife. To start with at least. He produced the bottle of Glenfiddich from his briefcase. It was her favourite malt whisky.

'Can I come in for a moment and talk?'

'What about?' Her eyes were on the bottle.

'Money,' he said. 'And what I might be able to do for you.'

'Oh, I see.' Her tone changed. 'Yes, come in then.'

Edgar followed her down the hall and into the kitchen. 'First things first,' he said, taking two tumblers from the cabinet. He opened the freezer, dropped ice cubes into the glasses then unscrewed the whisky bottle and poured in generous measures of spirit. She followed his movements with wary eyes.

'Quite finished making yourself at home?' she asked with asperity.

'Old habits die hard.' He handed her a glass. 'Cheers.'

She nodded and took a mouthful, swilling the whisky round her mouth appreciatively.

Sipping his own drink, he regarded her over the top of the glass. She had a healthy tan and looked slimmer than

144

he remembered. He resented the improvement in her appearance.

'The police have been questioning my mother about the murder of that man Dennison,' he said.

'Oh? Why?'

'She was at the pub in Great Horkesley at the same time as him on the night he was killed.'

'Really? What was she doing there?'

'Handing over blackmail money,' he said, watching her closely. There was a change in her expression. Alarm? Or guilt?

'What could anyone blackmail your mother about?'

'Some skeleton in her past. The blackmail is still going on and the police are trying to find out who it is.'

Valerie took another mouthful of her drink. 'Why are you telling me this?'

He kept his eyes on her face and his tone neutral. 'The thing is, Val, do you remember saying you'd screw me and my family for every penny you could get?'

She looked frightened and he felt a tingle of anticipation. He'd have to be careful how he killed her, though. An ex-husband was an obvious target for investigation.

He blocked her path as she put down her glass and moved towards the door. 'Get away from me!' she cried.

'You phoned me two days ago, you bitch,' he said menacingly.

'You're mad! I was on holiday. I've been on a Caribbean cruise for the last six weeks. It's the first decent holiday I've had in years.'

She saw his expression change, and stared at him. 'You didn't come here to talk about money at all. You thought I was blackmailing your mother and you came here to frighten me. You like that. You always did.' She was breathing hard. 'You rotten sod!' she shouted, and threw the rest of her whisky in his face.

The spirit stung his eyes. He lunged forward and slapped her face. In an explosion of frustration he began punching her . . . punishing her for divorcing him . . . and not being the blackmailer so he could end it by beating her to death. Just in time, he regained control and stood back.

She cowered away from him, wrapping her arms round her bruised body. 'You shouldn't have done that, Edgar,' she said venomously through a split lip. 'You really shouldn't.'

'Neither should you,' he snarled and stormed out.

There was only one thing to be done now, he thought savagely. And it had to be done quickly.

CHAPTER 17

'Mr Clark is on leave for two days,' a clerk told Scobie when he phoned Kenneth Clark's office the next morning.

No one else, it seemed, could provide Arthur Turnbull's last known address because Clark had the only key to the security cabinet where the HORSA membership records were kept. Scobie left a message for him to phone him on his return.

When Millson arrived in his office a DC from the incident room was waiting to see him with a computer print-out. The DC had used a search program to scan the data file of witnesses' statements from the Oak Tree pub to see if any of them mentioned a silver Volvo Estate. One did.

'Three of the vehicles reported in the car park didn't belong to any of the witnesses who came forward, sir,' he explained to Millson. 'The Volvo was one of them. The other two were the murdered man's Lotus Esprit and a Peugeot 505 which we now know belonged to Mrs Labram.'

'Well done,' Millson said.

'And I don't think the Volvo could have been there for very long, sir.'

Millson raised an eyebrow at him. 'What makes you think that?'

'The other cars were noticed by several witnesses, as you'd expect. Only one person reported seeing the Volvo Estate. Which suggests it was only there a short time. And if it was the same vehicle outside Dennison's flat, it probably followed him home.'

Millson nodded. 'Smart work.'

In Landermere Creek that evening, on board his yacht, *Consuelo*, Michael Labram made preparations for departure.

He loved night sailing. There was a magic about it. The hiss of the bow wave as it foamed white against the black water, leaving behind a phosphorescent wake. The muttering expanse of sail above, ghostly grey in the gloom. There was an excitement too, a sensation of racing through the night because a yacht's speed was exaggerated in the dark.

It was a pleasure he would have liked to share. Time was when Edgar would have come with him, but he was too busy with his practice these days. And Abby didn't really care for sailing. She was very good about his trips though, never a murmur of complaint over the amount of time he spent away from her.

He switched on the light above the chart table and cast an eye over the course he'd selected for tonight's sail down the Wallet to the Blackwater. He'd sailed the route many times before, but mostly in daylight.

On the first leg of the course along Pye Sands there were no light buoys to mark the channel, but it was straight and he knew it well. Once he'd located the Pye End buoy in the dark, a course of 160° would take him across an open stretch of water until he raised the white, five-second flash of the Medusa. After the Medusa buoy, a course of 230° would take him safely down the Wallet to the Knoll and the entrance to the Blackwater.

He heard the buzz of an approaching outboard engine and stepped up on deck as a dinghy came alongside. The bulky figure crouched in the stern reached out a hand and slipped the painter over one of the yacht's stern cleats. The outboard died.

He peered at the man clambering aboard. 'Edgar! What are you doing here?'

'Hullo, Dad.' Edgar Labram smiled at the man who thought he was his father. 'I thought I'd keep you

148

company and crew for you. You're always nagging me to come sailing again.'

'Oh, good. Why didn't you say so before, though?'

'Snap decision. I've had a bad day at the office and when Mother said you were off for a night sail I thought that's just what I need to calm me down.'

'So she knows you're with me?'

Edgar turned away to haul a rucksack from the dinghy. 'Oh yes, she knows,' he lied. 'I've brought my office suit along. I thought you could put me ashore at Brightlingsea tomorrow morning and I can walk up to the office.'

'Right. We'd better take the dinghy with us then.'

'Definitely,' said Edgar. That was essential to his plan. As was telling his mother he wouldn't be in to dinner tonight and would be late home.

Ten minutes later Edgar slipped *Consuelo*'s mooring. With Mike Labram at the helm they puttered along Landermere Creek and into Hamford Water under power. Beyond Island Point they hoisted sail, shut off the engine, and picked up the light offshore breeze to Pye End buoy.

In three-quarters of an hour *Consuelo* was bearing down on the flashing light of the Medusa buoy. 'Want to take the helm for a bit, Edgar?' Mike Labram asked.

Edgar glanced at the distance log and then the green glow of the compass. Mike would soon have to tack and change course. 'After we've tacked,' he said.

He went below, unzipped his rucksack, and transferred the wooden mallet he'd brought with him to the pouch of his sailing jacket. He returned on deck.

Minutes later Mike Labram called, 'Ready about!' and pushed the tiller to leeward, ducking his head in readiness for the boom swinging across.

Edgar turned away as though to release the jib sheet from its winch, and pulled the mallet from his pocket. Mike Labram was looking upwards at the mainsail, absorbed in the manoeuvre. Edgar turned swiftly, mallet raised, and hit him hard on the side of the head.

As the stricken man slumped down against the cabin

hatchway, Edgar pocketed the mallet, seized the tiller and pulled it hard over. He'd deliberately left the jib sheet secured so that as the boom swung across, the jib came aback and the yacht was hove-to, nodding gently in the slight swell.

Edgar peered into the wall of black around *Consuelo*. Only the occasional flash of the Medusa light buoy broke the darkness. Stooping, he dragged Mike Labram's unconscious body from the shallow cockpit onto the deck. *Consuelo* had a flush deck and no lifelines. He rolled the body across the deck and pushed it overboard then knelt there, watching and listening. After the initial splash the only sound was the lapping of water against the hull.

He scrambled into the cockpit, lifted the torch from its clip on the bulkhead and shone it around on the dark water. Nothing. Edgar's lips parted in a smile of satisfaction. He'd wondered, as they set off, if Mike would put on a lifejacket, in which case he would have had to push his head under until he drowned. In the conditions of a calm sea and a light wind, though, Mike hadn't bothered.

Edgar replaced the torch and freed the jib sheet. *Consuelo* came head to wind with her sails flapping. He collected his rucksack from the cabin and took a last look round to make sure he'd set the scene correctly. To all appearances Mike Labram had been hit on the head by the swinging boom as he tacked and been knocked overboard. Satisfied, Edgar climbed over the yacht's pushpit and into the dinghy.

He unzipped a compartment of the rucksack and took out a grid compass. Setting it to 325° he started the outboard. While Mike was helming, Edgar had bent over the chart table and laid off a return course from the Medusa. It was a course that would take him over the Naze Ledge to Stone Point and then to the short cut across Pye Sands that was only navigable by dinghies and vessels of shallow draft.

Two and a half hours after leaving Spencers and telling his mother he was visiting a client, Edgar Labram was back in his room. He'd secured his inheritance once and for all.

Early the following morning a fisherman trawling in Goldmer Gat saw a yacht in the distance behaving erratically, her sails alternately backing and filling. The next time he hauled his nets he changed course and went to investigate. Finding no one aboard, and her navigation lights switched on, he radioed Walton coastguard and reported the yacht's name, *Consuelo*, and her position.

The coastguard organized an air and sea search of the area for survivors and an hour later a helicopter spotted Michael Labram's body washed up on Gunfleet Sands where the tide had carried it during the night. The body was winched aboard the helicopter. Soon after, the inshore rescue boat reached *Consuelo* and took her in tow to Shotley.

A wallet on the body, and papers aboard the yacht, established the dead man's identity. The coastguard phoned Abigail Labram and reported the discovery of her husband's body. It looked as though he'd fallen, or been knocked, overboard from the yacht during the night, they told her.

A distressed Abigail phoned Edgar at his office in Brightlingsea and told him the news. 'I'll come home at once,' he said.

Driving to Spencers, Edgar rehearsed how he would respond to his mother's grief. He had no feelings about Mike Labram's death, no feelings at all. It had been like killing a stranger. When he arrived home he was able to comfort his mother with apparent sincerity. As far as Edgar was concerned she'd lost a husband who was nothing to do with him.

Kenneth Clark phoned Scobie two days later. Arthur Turnbull had been living in Harwich when he attended the reunion last November, he told Scobie. After he died,

John Dennison had simply written 'Died January 1991' on the card and filed it in the dead records.

'Is that all you can tell me?' Scobie asked. 'What about family?'

'I'm afraid that kind of information was in the file John had in his flat. The one that's missing.'

'To think this was once a thriving seaport,' Scobie commented as Millson drove along the neglected High Street in Harwich. 'Nelson put in here for the night once to escape the French, you know. They lay in wait for him outside the harbour and the locals told him there was no other way out. But he set off across Stone Banks and found one and it's been called the Medusa Channel ever since – after the name of his ship.'

'Really?' Millson was less interested in naval history than in locating Arthur Turnbull's last address. He found the street he was looking for and turned into it.

The address was a rented flat in a run-down terrace of houses. The present occupant had moved in recently and knew nothing about the previous tenant. One of the neighbours, an elderly woman in slippers and sagging tights, was more helpful. Turnbull, she told them, was a morose, ill-tempered old man who lived alone and had no visitors.

'None at all?' Scobie queried.

She shook her head. 'A girl called a few times. She was from Social, though.'

'What happened when he died?' Millson asked. 'Someone must have shown up then?'

'Nah. He collapsed in the street, see. Down by the harbour. Someone called the ambulance and he was took off to hospital. Next thing I heard he was dead.'

'Didn't anyone come and collect his things?'

'Yeah, 'bout a week later I see a van turn up – house-clearance people it was. They had keys an' took everything away. Never see'd anyone else there.'

152

Millson thanked the woman and they returned to the car.

'Sounds as though he didn't have any family,' Scobie said.

'Somebody must have registered the death,' Millson said. 'Let's find out who.'

Earlier that day Mike Labram's brother and family arrived at Spencers to give comfort and support to his widow. Edgar took the opportunity to return to his office in Brightlingsea for a while to clear up any urgent work requiring his attention.

Edgar felt at peace. There was a bright future ahead and his brain was busy with plans. He would sell his solicitor's practice and take a world cruise . . . perhaps take his secretary, Tracey, with him. Though he wasn't sure she'd be suitable given his new status as master of Spencers. Probably best to keep her on the side and look round for a woman of class to be mistress of the place.

The call came through in the middle of the afternoon. Edgar had been so wrapped up in his plans he'd almost forgotten that disembodied voice would be phoning again with instructions.

'Have you got the money?'

'No. There's been a terrible accident. Michael Labram is dead and my mother and I are very upset. Now go away and leave us alone. I don't want to hear from you ever again. It's over. D'you hear?' He slammed down the phone.

It rang again a few minutes later. 'It's not over,' the voice said. 'I still want the money.'

Edgar laughed down the phone. 'Mike can't alter his will now.'

'No, but you can go to prison for the murder of John Dennison.'

Edgar went cold. 'Rubbish! I don't know what you're talking about.'

'You followed your mother to the Oak Tree that night.

153

I was *there*. I saw you. Then you followed John Dennison home and killed him.'

The room swam as the voice went on, 'If I tell the police what I know they'll question you and you'll be finished. If you don't pay up you'll be in a police cell within the week. Do you understand?'

'Yes.' Edgar forced the word through closed teeth.

'Good. The same arrangement as before, then. Address the money to yourself at Spencers and a courier will call at your office midday tomorrow to collect.'

Edgar put down the phone and pounded the desk with his fist in rage.

The superintendent registrar in Colchester came out of his office to deal with the inquiry personally when Millson made himself known.

'January, you say, Chief Inspector?' He took down one of the heavy volumes from a rack and placed it on the table. 'January's our busiest month, you know,' he confided. 'They seem to hang on till Christmas and then . . . poof . . . down they go like ninepins. It's the cold weather, I suppose. What was the name of the deceased?'

'Arthur Turnbull,' Millson said.

The registrar opened the register and began turning the pages. 'Turnbull . . . Ah, here we are . . .' He stood aside to let Millson see.

Millson looked at the entry for Arthur Turnbull, his eye fastening on 'Name of informant'. He drew in his breath sharply.

'Oh, my God,' he said.

Scobie stepped forward and peered over his shoulder. *Sarah Howarth*, he read and under the box headed 'Qualification', the word *Stepdaughter*.

CHAPTER 18

For a year after her mother died, the only contact between
Sarah Howarth and her stepfather had been an occasional
exchange of letters. Then unexpectedly, after he'd moved
to Harwich, he asked her to come and see him. Reluc-
tantly, she drove over from Ipswich one evening after
work.

He appeared pleased to see her and insisted she stayed
to supper. Afterwards, as she was leaving, he said, 'I know
you got nothing when your mum died, Sarah, but I want
you to know I'll make it up to you when I go. All I ask
is you visit me sometimes. It's lonely living on your own
in this dump.'

He looked old and pathetic and Sarah no longer found
him frightening. He wasn't asking much and, since he was
going to leave her his money, it seemed a fair exchange.
Also he was getting on, she told herself, and she probably
wouldn't have to do it for long.

'OK, I don't mind popping in now and again,' she said.

Some months later he learned he had cancer and she
felt sorry for him. She visited him more frequently, calling
in after work and sometimes preparing a meal for him.

'You're a good girl, Sarah,' he told her one time, 'and
you'll get your reward when I'm gone. I've made a will
leaving everything to you.'

She didn't think he had a lot of money, but she hoped
it would be enough for a deposit on a little flat of her
own.

Then, one afternoon in January on his way to the post
office to collect his pension, Arthur Turnbull had a heart

attack. He died in the ambulance on the way to hospital.

As soon as the hospital phoned her and broke the news, Sarah went to his flat to look for the will.

When she found it she discovered he'd lied to her.

Immediately after the phone call, a wild-eyed Edgar Labram told his secretary to take the rest of the day off.

'I'm too upset to work,' he said.

Tracey went home believing her boss to be in deep shock over the death of his father. She mistook the suffused face and staring eyes for signs of grief.

Alone in his office, Edgar restlessly paced the floor. He was raging. After all his efforts, all the risks he'd taken, his inheritance was to be drained from him by never-ending demands from the voice on the phone.

He forced himself to calm down and to think. Was it a man? Was it a woman? He didn't know and he had no idea where to start finding out. Unless . . . His mother had asked the police if it could have been one of Arthur Turnbull's family who was blackmailing her. The police had discounted it and so had he at the time because his suspicions had been fixed on his ex-wife.

Who was this Arthur Turnbull? Presumably someone in his mother's past and known to Dennison. Edgar unlocked his safe and took out the file he'd brought away from John Dennison's flat. He sat down at his desk and started to read through it. It contained notes and file copies of letters written by Dennison. The letters were mainly about a reunion last year. As he was leafing through them, the name Arthur Turnbull leapt out at him. It was in a letter of condolence to a Sarah Howarth on the death of her stepfather.

Edgar straightened in his chair. Sarah Howarth. He'd seen the name somewhere. Then he remembered. Her name had been mentioned in newspaper reports of Dennison's murder. Sarah Howarth was Dennison's girl-friend! And she was this man Turnbull's stepdaughter!

Edgar Labram's eyes gleamed with excitement. *She* was

Dennison's accomplice, not that Wilson woman. *It was Sarah Howarth who was blackmailing him*!

Edgar whimpered with emotion . . . a confusion of rage, relief and pleasure. His eye fell on the address in the letter. Ipswich.

He replaced the file in the safe and took out his gun.

There had been plenty of drink at the reunion in the Wessex Hotel in Bournemouth and Arthur Turnbull had enjoyed himself. He recognized faces he hadn't seen for fifty years and looked around for Abby Coran. He wanted to see her again and stimulate his memory of spoiling her for Mike Labram.

He saw Midge Wilson animatedly chatting with a group of women and took her aside to ask about Abby. 'Abby Coran? She didn't want to come,' Midge said. She was swaying on her feet, gripping her glass carelessly.

'She married, I suppose?' he asked casually.

'Yes, she married Mike Labram. It was very sudden . . . they'd only just met at that party at Larnaca.' Her speech was slurred.

'Any children?'

'Only the one. A boy. Edgar.'

She leaned closer to him, putting a finger to the side of her nose. 'Had him just over seven months later,' she breathed.

'I see.' He felt the stir of excitement.

He brought her another drink and edged her into a corner away from the others. 'Tell me more,' he invited.

He soon wheedled out of a befuddled Midge that Abby Coran discovered she was pregnant soon after he'd violated her. The child must be his. Arthur was amused and curious.

Before he left, Arthur obtained Abby's address from John Dennison and learned in conversation with him that her son, Edgar, was a solicitor and lived at Spencers with her and Mike.

A week later Arthur Turnbull drove down to Beaumont

cum Moze and spent the day spying on Spencers with binoculars. He sniggered when he brought Edgar into focus and saw a likeness to himself at that age. Then he saw Abby . . . matronly, and still attractive.

A month after the reunion Arthur Turnbull was told the tumour in his bowels was inoperable and was growing fast. It was a death sentence. Some people in like circumstances endeavour to make amends for their past sins and to perform good deeds in the time they have left. Arthur Turnbull was not one of them. Arthur had an overwhelming urge to wreak havoc on the lives of those left behind. It anaesthetized his pain and suffering working out a way to satisfy that urge – one that would enable him to ravage his victims from beyond the grave.

Sarah had found the handwritten will in a drawer and with it a letter. Arthur had been about to deposit them with his bank for safe-keeping.

The will was short and simple. Arthur Turnbull left everything he possessed to his natural son, Edgar Labram of Spencers, Beaumont cum Moze, Essex.

Sarah was devastated. She hadn't known Artie had a son. He'd conned her, let her believe he had no one else but her. Her feelings of betrayal turned to fury. She would destroy the will! No one would know. She still wouldn't get anything, of course, because she wasn't related to him and without a will he'd be intestate and the money would go to the Crown.

The letter was addressed to Edgar Labram. In it, Arthur wrote that he'd once had a passionate affair with Edgar's mother, Abby Coran. Arthur had enjoyed describing an imaginary romance with Abby. The letter ended by explaining that Arthur had only discovered at a recent reunion that Edgar was his son and he thought Edgar should know who his father was.

Reading the letter, Sarah saw a ray of hope. If she explained the situation to this Edgar Labram he might offer her a share of the money. Anyway, there was no harm in asking and the address wasn't far away. She would drive over there with the will and the letter and plead with him.

When she found the address was a country mansion she was taken aback and parked her car in the road outside. While she was debating what to do, a Volvo Estate scrunched down the drive and halted at the roadside. The driver turned his head to look along the road and Sarah tensed with fear. The man was a lookalike of her stepfather as she first remembered him. The Estate turned into the road and drove away. Sarah started her car and followed it.

In Brightlingsea High Street, the Volvo turned onto the forecourt of some offices and the driver got out and went inside. Sarah glanced at the brass nameplate on the door pillar and saw the name Edgar Labram. Well, that settled it. Not that she'd had much doubt once she'd seen him. He was exactly like Artie and she was quite sure he wouldn't allow her a share of the money.

On the way home she called in at an undertaker's to make arrangements for the funeral.

'Is it to be a burial or a cremation?' the man asked.

In his will Arthur had specified that he was to be buried. 'Burn him,' she told the shocked undertaker. 'It's what he deserves.'

At the crematorium a few days later, John Dennison was the only person to attend the funeral apart from the undertaker's men and herself.

'I'm the secretary of the Retired Staff Association from your stepfather's old department,' he explained as he introduced himself.

Afterwards, he invited her to lunch and over the meal he spoke of the reunion he'd organized the previous November. 'Your stepfather was there, you know, and he really enjoyed himself,' he said, searching for words to cheer Sarah in her lone bereavement.

'You don't have to comfort me,' Sarah said. 'I hated him and I'm glad he's dead. Go on about the reunion

Artie went to. Did he meet some people called Labram there?'

'No, they didn't come. I know them, though. I've met the husband, Michael. He's a near millionaire. They have a country estate in Essex.'

That was when it registered with Sarah that Artie's bastard son had a wealthy family and there might be a way of redressing the wrong Artie had done her.

As they parted after lunch John Dennison asked if he might see her again.

Sarah smiled. Why not? He was friendly and pleasant and she liked him. 'Yes, ring me,' she said.

Over the next few weeks she worked out a scheme. It was clear from Artie's letter that Edgar and Michael Labram were unaware of Edgar's origins. And Abigail Labram certainly wouldn't want them to find out. Sarah shied away from the word 'blackmail'. She would merely recoup what was rightfully hers. Artie had promised her the money and she'd earned it too with her visits, pampering and comforting him.

She totted up his savings in investments and building society accounts and they came to fifteen thousand pounds. That was the amount she would levy from Edgar Labram's family. It wasn't blackmail, Sarah told herself; it was siphoning off a minuscule portion of Artie's son's future inheritance and he wouldn't even miss it.

The idea for disguising her voice came to Sarah at a children's birthday party. One of the children had a toy microphone for Karaoke singing. It distorted and amplified the voice. Sarah bought one and used it when she phoned Abigail Labram. She only asked for five thousand pounds as she thought Mrs Labram would be more inclined to pay the smaller amount than fifteen thousand all at once.

She'd anticipated Abigail Labram would insist Edgar was her husband's son and told her she'd had DNA tests carried out which proved he wasn't. She hadn't, but she knew they could be done with hairs from Artie and Edgar at a cost of two hundred pounds. The bluff was sufficient and Abigail Labram caved in.

Sarah thought her plan for the handover of the money was foolproof. John Dennison was now dating her regularly and as a girl drinking alone in a pub was conspicuous and would be remembered, she decided to use him as cover. She arranged to meet him in the Oak Tree at nine o'clock that evening, well before Mrs Labram would arrive with the money.

Sarah expected to be sitting in the bar, drinking with John. If all was well, she would visit the toilet, slip outside in the dark, collect the money from Mrs Labram's car and return to her seat without anyone being the wiser.

The plan went wrong because John hadn't turned up when Mrs Labram drove in to the Oak Tree car park at 9.15. Sarah was still sitting in her car waiting for him. She saw the Peugeot being reversed into the vacant space next to her and hunched down in her seat to escape notice.

As Abigail Labram walked into the pub, Sarah jumped out, opened the door of the Peugeot, took the envelope and returned to her car. Starting the engine, she headed for the exit.

As she paused there, a silver Volvo drove in. She glanced at it and then at the driver caught in the glare of her headlights. It was Edgar Labram. Realizing he must have followed his mother's car, Sarah drove away fast, heading for Ipswich.

Behind her, John Dennison's Lotus swept into the car park from the opposite direction and parked in the space Sarah had just vacated next to the Peugeot.

Later in the evening an annoyed John Dennison phoned Sarah and demanded to know why she'd stood him up.

She made an excuse. 'I didn't. I was ill.'

'Oh? When I phoned you from the Oak Tree at a quarter to ten there was no reply.'

She improvised. 'I was at the chemist's buying medicine.'

'Well, if you knew you couldn't come why didn't you phone and say so before I left?'

He went on arguing and Sarah became angry because the fault was his through being late and she couldn't say so. In the end she said, 'Get lost!' and put down the phone.

As they left the registrar's office Millson said in exasperation, 'I was looking at this the wrong way round. Turnbull wasn't being blackmailed by Dennison. He was the source of Dennison's information – or rather his stepdaughter was. She must have found out Abigail's secret when Turnbull died – probably from his papers or letters. Dennison would have met her at the funeral – the secretary attends all the funerals. They chatted, I expect. She trots out her stepdad's secret, he tells her how wealthy the Labrams are and they decide to blackmail Mrs Labram.'

Scobie nodded. 'Sarah Howarth phoned Mrs Labram and made the demand and Dennison picked up the money.'

'That's about it and I'll bet it was her he was trying to phone from the pub and having the row with later when he got home. They must have quarrelled – perhaps over the split of the money. Then he went downstairs and consoled himself with Irene Smedley.'

'But in that case, who killed him?'

'I've said all along there has to be another victim besides Abigail Labram. And Sarah Howarth knows who it is. She must have found other dirt among Turnbull's effects.' He looked at his watch. 'We'll get a search warrant in the morning and bring her in for questioning.'

Sarah Howarth left work looking forward to a quiet evening at home poring over the particulars of flats an estate agent had sent her. Tomorrow, she would collect her final five thousand pounds and start looking for a new flat.

At first, she'd been confused by the murder of John Dennison. At the back of her mind was a nagging fear

162

Edgar Labram had killed him, though she could see no reason why he should. In the following weeks she studied the reports and the comments made by the police, looking for an explanation of the murder. There was none.

Then, last week, there was an appeal for the driver of a silver Volvo Estate seen near John's house at the time of the murder. And then she knew for sure Edgar Labram was a murderer.

Her phone call to him today had provided further proof. He'd only agreed to pay when she threatened to tell the police he'd killed John. She shivered. After she'd collected the money tomorrow she would ring the police.

At nine o'clock that evening Edgar Labram told his mother he was going to visit a client again and would be late back. Then he loaded his revolver and set off for Sarah Howarth's address in Ipswich.

CHAPTER 19

Valerie Labram had had a hard day. She carried her evening meal into the sitting room on a tray and sat down wearily in front of the television. She deeply resented having to work to keep up the payments on the mortgage with which her ex-husband had saddled her.

The regional news was on and the announcer was repeating an item she'd heard before about the murder of a man called John Dennison. As she reached for the remote control to change to another channel her attention was caught by the next words.

'The police are again appealing for information about the driver of a silver Volvo Estate seen near the murdered man's house in Mile End Road, Colchester, that evening.'

Valerie continued munching a buttered roll, turning the words over in her mind. Edgar had a silver Volvo Estate. She saw a way to pay him back for hitting her the other evening. He'd turn blue if the police came to his office and started questioning him. She buttered herself another roll. Come to think of it, it might even have been him sitting there in his car. It would be just like him to put the frighteners on some poor woman by sitting outside her house late at night. She hoped this could stir up a load of trouble for him. And serve him right.

She put down her tray and went to the phone.

George Millson too was watching television. Or rather, his daughter was watching a pop group gyrating and wailing and he was waiting for the next programme about a new criminal justice bill.

As the strident voices and twanging guitars faded and the end captions started rolling, the doorbell rang.

'I'll get it,' Dena said. 'I expect it's Julie.'

She returned, looking disappointed. 'It's Copperknob,' she said.

Rising to his feet, Millson said severely, 'I've told you before, don't call Sergeant Scobie Copperknob.'

'He doesn't mind.'

'No, but I do.' He went out to the hall. 'What's up, Norris?'

'A Valerie Labram has rung in and said she thinks the man in the silver Volvo was her ex-husband.'

'Edgar Labram?'

'Yes. She lives in Sudbury. I thought you'd want to see her straightaway.'

'Dead right I do,' Millson said, reaching for his coat.

'You!' Sarah Howarth started back in fright as she opened her door and saw Edgar Labram.

Her recognition of him was the proof Edgar Labram needed. As she tried to close the door, he thrust it back in her face, twirled her round and clamped a hand over her mouth. Kicking the door to behind him, he pulled out his gun and held it against her head.

'Make a sound and you're dead!' he snarled and threw her forwards onto a sofa.

She tried to bluff. 'I don't know who you are – I thought you were someone else. What do you want?'

'Don't play the innocent with me, you blackmailing bitch! You've had ten thousand pounds from me and my mother and you thought you were getting another five thousand tomorrow.'

She gazed up at him fearfully. 'I – I'll pay you back. Please . . . let me explain. I was only—'

'Save your breath and tell me how you know I'm not Mike Labram's son?'

'Because your real father was my stepfather, Arthur Turnbull.'

165

'That's a lie! My father was an airman. He was killed in the war.'

'No, I've told you the truth. He left a will and a letter that said so. I've still got them.' A thought came to her. Salvation. 'Look, you can still file probate and pick up the fifteen thousand he left you. He promised to leave the money to me, and that's why—'

She broke off as he raised the gun, his finger on the trigger. 'Shut your lying mouth or I'll kill you like I killed your boyfriend!'

'He had nothing to do with the blackmail! He didn't even know about it.'

'You're lying again!'

'Why should I lie? You killed an innocent man.'

'If I did, it was your fault. They're all your fault.'

They? Sarah went cold. 'How many people have you killed?'

'You'll be the fifth,' he said. 'And I shall enjoy killing you.' His mouth was working angrily, his face distorted. 'I'm going to make you suffer for what you've done to me.'

Sarah trembled. He sounded like Artie in one of his rages. 'You won't get away with it,' she said desperately.

'Oh, but I will. You'll see.' He gave a braying laugh, his eyes glaring at her insanely. 'You'll see,' he repeated.

'Abigail Labram insisted she hadn't told anyone about the blackmail,' Millson said, as Scobie turned off the bypass and onto the A134. 'But suppose she was lying – she lied about pretty well everything else – and told her son. Not about Arthur Turnbull – she wouldn't tell him that. I expect she spun him the yarn about the airman. The threat of losing a fortune like Michael Labram's would be a powerful incentive for Edgar Labram to commit murder.'

Scobie nodded. 'So, Edgar Labram follows his mother to the pub, sees Dennison pick up the money and follows him home and kills him.'

'That's the way I see it,' Millson said. 'And if his ex-wife

confirms it was him outside Dennison's house, we go and
pick him up.'

Valerie Labram was nervous as Millson started questioning her. She hadn't expected such a quick response to her
phone call, nor for it to be from the chief inspector in
charge of the murder investigation. She had expected
the police to call on Edgar and ask him embarrassing
questions. And here they were, questioning *her*.

'I only said I *thought* it might be Edgar's car, Chief
Inspector.'

'Quite so, Mrs Labram, but what did you think he was
doing there at that time of night?'

'Oh, probably hanging around some poor woman's
house and frightening her out of her wits.'

Millson frowned as he realized Valerie Labram wasn't
connecting her ex-husband with the murder. If Edgar
Labram had an alibi for his presence in Mile End Road
that night, then he was probably not the murderer.

'That's a strange thing to say. Do you have a reason for
saying it?' he asked.

'Yes. Edgar enjoys frightening people. That's why I
couldn't stand living with him any longer.' Her resent-
ment flared up and she went on angrily, 'He made my
life hell when he didn't get his own way. He even
threatened to kill me once. Said he'd "disappear" me.'

Scobie looked up from taking notes. 'What did he mean
by that?'

She laughed cynically. 'Bury me in a rubbish tip where
I wouldn't be found.'

'He sounds a violent man,' Millson said.

'You can say that again,' she said vehemently, anger
rising once more. 'He came here threatening me again
only last week. He accused me of blackmailing his mother
and knocked me about, the bastard.'

Millson's eyes lit up. 'He told you his mother was being
blackmailed?'

'Yes, that's what he said.'

167

Millson gave himself a mental thumbs up. Abigail Labram *had* told her son. Motive established.

'Why should he think it was you?' he asked curiously.

She looked uncomfortable. 'He cheated me over the divorce . . . left me with a horrendous mortgage. I said I'd make the family pay. I meant legally,' she added quickly. 'My solicitor said there was nothing I could do, though.'

Millson stood up. 'Well, thank you, Mrs Labram, you've been a great help.'

'These questions you've been asking me, Chief Inspector. Do they mean you suspect Edgar of killing that man?'

'I can't answer that. Our inquiries are not yet complete,' Millson said smoothly.

'If he did, I hope they shut him away for a long, long time,' she said.

'Beaumont cum Moze, Norris,' Millson ordered, snapping on his seat belt. 'We'll take him tonight.'

They were at Newton Green when the call came through on the car phone. Millson answered, listened for a moment, then snapped, 'Pull off the road, Norris!'

Scobie took a left turn into a side road and stopped.

'There's been a 999 call about a kidnapping in Ipswich,' Millson said. 'An hour ago a man forced a girl into a Volvo Estate and drove off. The address and description fit Sarah Howarth.'

'Labram?'

'Almost certainly. He's found out she and Dennison were in the blackmail together. Or perhaps she's been carrying on the blackmail herself.'

'Why kidnap her?' Scobie asked.

'Because he's going to "disappear" her.' Millson's face was grim in the glow of the dashboard. 'Get his ex-wife on the phone.'

Scobie pulled out his notebook, checked Valerie Labram's number and keyed it. When she answered he handed the phone to Millson.

'Mrs Labram, this is very important,' Millson said. 'I

want you to think carefully. When your husband threatened to bury you in a rubbish tip, did he mean any particular one?'

'Well, he was living here with me then, so he meant the waste site in Sudbury, I think. We sometimes took things there that wouldn't go in the dustbin. There's a machine there that'll gobble anything.'

'Where is this?'

'On the edge of town. There's a sign to it as you go out of Sudbury on the road to Halstead.'

'Thank you.' Millson turned to Scobie. 'A131 – other side of Sudbury – and step on it!' He opened the dashboard compartment and pulled out the handset. 'I'll call out the cavalry.'

At the waste site, Edgar Labram prodded Sarah in the back with the gun, forcing her up the concrete steps to the open hopper. He'd switched on the machine and left the safety door open. He chuckled. Soon now. Sarah heard him and shuddered.

He moved up beside her. Flicking on the torch, he shone it inside, illuminating the gleaming cavern.

'Look down there,' he said, pushing her forward.

Sarah looked down and saw the heaving steel walls and the piston moving backwards and forwards. Her legs gave way and she collapsed in a dead faint. Edgar growled in annoyance. He wanted her alive and kicking when he threw her in. Stooping over her, he prised up an eyelid to make sure she wasn't faking, then propped her against the side of the hopper and waited for her to recover.

CHAPTER 20

'Can't you go any faster?' Millson demanded as Scobie sped through Sudbury's deserted marketplace, headlamps on full beam, hazard lights flashing.

'Not if you want us to get there in one piece,' Scobie retorted.

'No sign of the troops,' Millson grumbled. 'I suppose they have to come in from the outback in this part of the world.'

Sarah Howarth's eyelids fluttered open. She came to and quickly closed them again. Where was he? Lifting her eyelids fractionally, she peered through narrow slits into the gloom, her head unmoving.

In front of her she saw his silhouette against the skyline. He was standing a few feet away with his back to her and holding the gun loosely, arm dangling at his side. She'd seen the weapon close to in the flat. It was a revolver, so it didn't need cocking – she knew that much – and she believed it didn't have a safety catch.

Opening her eyes fully, she cautiously drew up her legs and moved her body into a stooping position, muscles bunched to spring. Then, taking a breath, she leapt forward and grabbed at the gun.

She sobbed with relief as she crashed to the ground with it in her hands. Scrambling to her feet she pointed it at him.

He recovered from his surprise and advanced on her snarling, certain she wouldn't, or couldn't, use the weapon. Sarah quickly pointed the gun to the ground and, holding it firmly, squeezed the trigger. A bullet thudded against the concrete and whined away in a ricochet. She let out her breath. The gun might not have been loaded, or had a hidden safety catch.

She raised the barrel again. He was standing stock-still, looking at her fearfully. If I hand him over to the police, Sarah thought, I'll be arrested too. For blackmail. And it'll be goodbye to ten thousand pounds. But if . . .

He backed away as she moved towards him. 'Now . . . *you* walk up those steps and look down inside,' she said.

The rumbling machinery masked the sound of Scobie's car approaching until it roared into the compound and screeched to a halt. In the glare of the headlights, they saw Sarah Howarth on the steps to the hopper holding a gun. There was no sign of Edgar Labram. She turned, shielding her eyes with one hand and pointing the gun at them with the other.

'Oh, hell!' Millson groaned. 'And we've no armed backup.' He jumped from the car, stooping behind the open door to shield himself.

'Police!' he shouted. 'Drop the gun, Sarah.'

To his surprise and relief she bent down, laid the gun carefully at her feet, straightened and raised her hands.

Scobie ran forward, followed by Millson. As they came nearer, they saw a figure cringing in the shadows on the lower step.

Edgar Labram staggered to his feet as Scobie picked up the gun. 'She was going to kill me!' he sobbed. 'She was just about to push me into that machine!'

Sarah Howarth said, 'No, I wasn't, I was just giving him a fright.'

Millson looked at her. Her face, white in the headlights, had a deceptive, slightly vacant expression.

'Anyway,' she said, lowering her hands, 'you'll need my evidence to convict him. He's killed four people, you know.'

'*Four*?' Scobie queried.

'John, Marjorie Wilson, a man called Smedley and Michael Labram. He told me about them. And he was going to kill me too. So you see, you'll need my help.'

'She's got a nerve, telling us we need her help,' Scobie said, as they followed the cavalcade of police cars leaving the waste site.

A number of cars had converged on the site in response to Millson's call and Edgar Labram and Sarah Howarth had been arrested and were on their way to Colchester police station in separate cars.

Millson said wryly, 'She's right though.'

'*Was* she going to kill him, d'you think?'

'That, Norris, is something we'll never know,' Millson said.

It was three o'clock in the morning when George Millson eventually arrived home. A sleepy-eyed Dena was squatting at the foot of the stairs.

'I was worried,' she said. 'You don't usually bog off for half the night without ringing me.'

'I'm sorry, I was busy. Have you been sitting here all alone?'

'No, Julie was here till two and we played records.'

Julie prowling his house in the small hours was not something Millson cared to dwell on. 'You know, I don't think Julie is suitable company for you, Dena.'

'Dad, her father's a High Court judge.'

He snorted derisively. 'She told you that?'

'It's true! His name's Babergh. I looked him up in your *Who's Who.*'

There was no answer to that. Millson laughed and tousled her hair.